GRIMOIRE
The Curse of the Midions

by Brad Strickland

SLEUTH

DIAL

DIAL BOOKS FOR YOUNG READERS
A division of Penguin Young Readers Group
Published by The Penguin Group
Penguin Group (USA) Inc., 375 Hudson Street,
New York, NY 10014, U.S.A.
Penguin Group (Canada), 90 Eglinton Avenue East, Suite 700,
Toronto, Ontario, Canada M4P 2Y3 (a division of Pearson Penguin Canada Inc.)
Penguin Books Ltd, 80 Strand, London WC2R 0RL, England
Penguin Ireland, 25 St. Stephen's Green, Dublin 2, Ireland
(a division of Penguin Books Ltd)
Penguin Group (Australia), 250 Camberwell Road,
Camberwell, Victoria 3124, Australia
(a division of Pearson Australia Group Pty Ltd)
Penguin Books India Pvt Ltd, 11 Community Centre,
Panchsheel Park, New Delhi - 110 017, India
Penguin Group (NZ), Cnr Airborne and Rosedale Roads, Albany,
Auckland 1310, New Zealand (a division of Pearson New Zealand Ltd)
Penguin Books (South Africa) (Pty) Ltd, 24 Sturdee Avenue,
Rosebank, Johannesburg 2196, South Africa
Penguin Books Ltd, Registered Offices: 80 Strand, London WC2R 0RL, England

Book designed by Jasmin Rubero
Text set in Centaur MT
Printed in the U.S.A.
1 3 5 7 9 10 8 6 4 2

Library of Congress Cataloging-in-Publication Data
Strickland, Brad.
Grimoire : the curse of the Midions / by Brad Strickland.
p.   cm.
Summary: In London with his parents, twelve-year-old Jarvey Midion is introduced to
the Grimoire, a powerful book of spells that transports him to a strange place
and time where danger lurks around every corner.
ISBN 0-8037-3060-8
[1. Fantasy. 2. Time and space—Fiction. 3. Magic—Fiction.] I. Title.
PZ7.S9166Gr 2006
[Fic]—dc22
2005034059

For Rebecca,
who loves tales of enchantment

Table of Contents

CHAPTER I
Welcome to Ḥag's Court

Jarvis Midion was worn out after the long, long overnight airplane flight from Atlanta to London. His head ached from the rattling of the Underground car into which his family trooped early in the morning. Usually Jarvey was most cheerful in the morning, but lack of sleep made him crabby. Now he had the grumpy thought that the three of them were marching along the sidewalk like a pathetic circus parade with their suitcases trundling along behind them. "There it is," his father said, pointing to a building ahead. It stood in the dark corner of London called Hag's Court.

It wasn't much of a hotel, in Jarvey's opinion. It was a weather-beaten brick building, with a pub on the ground floor. The pub's signboard showed a warped, dwarfish, leering creature over the name of the place, the Spriggan. The hotel itself didn't even have a lobby, just an odd-shaped nook with a counter where a chubby-faced woman with frazzled red hair had Jarvey's father sign the register.

"Just the three of you, then, ducks?" asked the woman with a smile that showed enormous front teeth.

"Just the three," his father agreed. "I'm Cadmus Midion, this is my wife, Samantha, and this guy here is our son, Jarvey. He's just turned twelve." He ruffled Jarvey's brownish blond hair, brushing it up into spikes, and Jarvey frowned in annoyance.

The woman looked startled, but then gave him a smile. "You're here on holiday, then?"

Jarvey's dad shook his head. "Business, and a sad business at that. Last week I received a letter telling me that my great-grandfather Thaddeus Midion had died in London, and we've flown over for the reading of the will."

"Oh, I'm so sorry. Very old, was he, then?"

"I honestly don't know," Jarvey's dad confessed. "To tell you the truth, I didn't even know I *had* a great-grandfather until the letter came. But I suppose he must have been pretty old. I'm thirty-four myself, so he couldn't have been very young!"

The woman turned around and fumbled inside a set of dark cubbyholes for a key. "Here we are," she said brightly. "I'll put you in rooms five and six, shall I? It's a lovely set, two bedrooms and between them a bath *en suite*, quite large. Let me lead you up to it, you'll never find it else." She chuckled. "We've lost Yanks in the mysterious winding halls. Some say it's the mischief of the Spriggan that misleads them!"

"What's a Spriggan?" Mrs. Midion asked curiously.

"Well, it's a kind of evil spirit, isn't it?" the woman replied with a chuckle. "Like a pixie, or sprite— like Puck in Shakespeare's play, you know. Causes mischief, the Spriggan does, sours milk, breaks

3

mirrors—with me, he steals my keys and lays them down just anywhere!"

Jarvey caught the quick, almost frightened look that his mother gave to his father. Mr. Midion pursed his lips and glanced at his son, silently shaking his head: *Don't say anything,* the look said.

The woman didn't notice any of this as she led them up a gloomy, narrow, twisting stair. They went around corners and past closed doors, struggling with their three suitcases, until she stopped at the very end of the passage. "Here we are!"

She unlocked the door of Number 5 and flattened herself against the wall so they could squeeze past. The room boasted a big canopy bed with a small round bedside table sporting a chunky white telephone and an old-fashioned wind-up alarm clock. A single narrow window looked out into the green branches of a tree.

"Bath is just through there, and the smaller bedroom is beyond it," the woman said. "Have a lovely time, then, and if you need anything at all, my name is Mrs. Macauley, but please call me Grace."

As soon as she had closed the door, Jarvey dropped his suitcase. "I wish I could have stayed home."

"You'll love London," Mrs. Midion said. She was just an inch taller than Jarvey, and her light brown hair looked frizzed and tired after the long flight. Her brown eyes pleaded with Jarvey to be pleasant.

"Maybe I've got a Spriggan following me," Jarvey returned.

"That's just superstition." His dad sounded very sure of himself.

"Then why am I always in trouble at school?" Jarvey asked.

"You're tired," Mrs. Midion said. "You should have slept on the plane. Go check out your room."

"Okay." Jarvey lugged his suitcase into the passage between the rooms and reported, "The bathroom's about the size of my closet!" The bedroom on the far side was half the size of his room at home. He set his suitcase down and walked back into his parents' room.

The tiny TV there was showing the morning news, with a blond man and a dark-haired lady soberly talking about cricket or something. "You'd better unpack," Mrs. Midion said. "Then please catch up on your sleep so you won't be so cranky when we go sightseeing."

"I don't want to sleep," Jarvey grumbled. He didn't add *because that's when the bad dreams come*, but the thought lingered in his mind.

"You're just grouchy because you're sleepy," his dad said.

His mom tried to smooth Jarvey's rusty brown hair, without much success. "Try to enjoy yourself," she said. "We have to go to the reading of the will tomorrow, and then we'll spend Friday, Saturday, and Sunday exploring London."

"But baseball tryouts are Friday," Jarvey said.

"Coach Brock knows you have to be away," his dad said. "Make the best of it."

"But I wanted to be the pitcher. After last season—"

"I know, I know," his father said. Dr. Midion put his hand on his son's shoulder. "You had some bad breaks after that one great game. But if I can give up teaching summer session, then you can give up a couple of days of baseball practice. Besides, we may get rich from this! What if my mysterious great-grandfather Thaddeus was an eccentric billionaire? Maybe when we get back I can even buy a baseball team!"

Jarvey grunted. His dad had an irritating way of being upbeat about everything. His dad loved to spend hours reading, but Jarvey always wanted to be outside, and he would rather be out on a baseball field than doing almost anything else. Odd things didn't happen on the baseball diamond—well, anyway, not so many of them.

Jarvey felt a yawn coming on and tried to stifle it, but that only made his jaw joints ache. Finally he couldn't keep it in. His mom chuckled. "Playing games all night on your GameMax."

"Did not," Jarvey muttered. "Power pack went dead halfway through Galactic Death Run 3000."

His father sighed. "Son, this is a golden opportunity for you. You can see a new city and maybe soak up a little bit of learning. This is London, Jarvey! This is where Shakespeare wrote his plays and George III planned the war against the Americans during the Revolution. Where Winston Churchill kept the country together even when the Germans were bombing it during World War II. It's a place of heroes and history, Jarvey! The Tower of London goes all the way back to Roman times. You won't find anything that old in Bayesville, Georgia!"

"What about the dirt?" Jarvey shot back. "I'll bet it's just as old as London dirt!"

His dad laughed. "I'll concede the point. But cheer up, son. It'll be fun. You'll see."

Jarvey couldn't help yawning again. While he had sat slumped by the dark window of the transatlantic jet, his mom and dad had snoozed away. Maybe they were right. Maybe if he slept for an hour or so he'd feel more human.

Back in his room, Jarvey kicked off his Nikes and peeled off socks, jeans, and red T-shirt. The shower sputtered out a thin stream of tepid water. He showered, then toweled off, pulled on some shorts and a clean white T-shirt with BAYESVILLE BOMBERS stenciled on it, and then slipped between the sheets.

He was asleep before he knew it.

One of the dreams came: The July day a year ago, when the Bombers were up against the Center Street Chargers, the day he was so angry.

In the dream, Jarvey felt a strange sense of dread.

It had happened halfway through the third inning. Once already he had struck out, and he had done a miserable job out in left field. His game was off that day. He had overrun an easy fly, missing it by five feet, and then had fielded a wildly bouncing grounder only to drop the ball.

The Charger pitcher was a tall, rangy kid with a mean face who grinned as Jarvey stepped up to bat. "Easy out!" the pitcher behind him had called.

Somehow the first two pitches, high and just inside the strike zone, flew by with no time passing. Jarvey didn't even hear the umpire call the strikes. The pitcher was winding up. Jarvey felt anger at himself building—what was wrong with him today? He should do better than this, should be able to—

Crack!

Something struck Jarvey in the face, hard enough to sting, and he heard everyone yelling. He stood dazed. The ball, the ball—

Was vanishing over the fence.

Jarvey became aware that he was holding the stump of the bat. The rest of it lay in shattered splinters.

"Run the bases," the umpire ordered, and Jarvey began the jog.

The first baseman gave him an unbelieving stare. "How'd you do that? I didn't even see you swing!"

Jarvey didn't answer. He couldn't. He had not swung.

His bat had exploded, and the ball had flown away. That wasn't the first time something strange had happened. In first grade, the class field day had been ruined by a steady, hard rain, and Jarvey had felt furious about not being able to go outside.

Then the classroom window had blown out, shattering into glittering shards, making Miss Daly scream in alarm. A suddenly pounding rain had whipped in on a cold wind. The class had to leave the classroom and go down to the cafeteria for the rest of the day.

Second grade, and Jarvey had been humiliated when he hadn't been able to spell a word at the board. The lights overhead had flared to incredible brightness, then had exploded, one after another, with tinkles of glass and puffs of smoke. Kids yelled and ducked under the desks. The whole school had lost power. The buses had come early that day.

But never had anything so disturbing happened outside, never on a baseball field.

In the dream, Jarvey's feet grew heavier and heavier as he tried to run the bases. He could barely move.

A crooked little monstrous creature waited at home plate.

"You're the Spriggan," Jarvey said, wondering how he even knew that word.

"No," the creature had said with an evil grin. "*You* are."

Jarvey's eyes jerked open, and he rolled out of bed, his heart beating hard. Then he realized that it had all been another dream, one of the dreams he had come to dread. He crawled back under the covers, trying to control his rapid breathing.

His parents always told him he was imagining things.

After the window incident, they had explained that his anger hadn't caused the window to shatter. It must have been the force of the wind, his dad had insisted. And the classroom lights had blown because of a short circuit, and his home run had just shown that he was stronger and quicker than he knew. Of course, he had played badly in every other game, because his nerves were on edge waiting for something else to happen. His parents reassured him after his bad dreams too: He was just keyed up, excited, upset. Dreams didn't mean anything.

Jarvey wanted to agree with them, because if they were right, he wasn't—well, crazy. Even though crazy things happened around him sometimes, and more than once his parents had been called to a conference at school, when water pipes burst in Jarvey's presence or every computer locked up as he sat at a keyboard. Although his teachers insisted that he didn't *do* anything, the principal always gave him suspicious looks.

The light coming in through the window had a late-afternoon redness. Jarvey got out of bed, still feeling shaky from the nightmare. He went into the tiny bathroom and washed his face in cold water. That helped a little. Staring into the mirror over the round sink, Jarvey gazed at his own face. His dark blue eyes looked back at him accusingly, and the spray of freckles across his nose reminded him of being out in the sun, playing baseball.

Jarvey sighed. He supposed he had been unfair to his dad. Sometimes he wondered if his father was disappointed in him. The two of them weren't much alike. Dr. Midion had dozens of awards on his shelves for his academic work, going all the way back to grade school. Jarvey was lucky to keep a C average, with a few B grades sprinkled in. And though his father always came to the games, he never seemed all that enthusiastic about baseball.

Jarvey returned to his room, got dressed, and then pushed through the connecting door to his parents' room. "Mom? Dad?" The room was empty.

Jarvey felt a little wave of uneasiness. Maybe he should go down to the lobby and see if what's her name, Grace Macauley, knew where his parents had gone.

The dark corridor was a baffling maze. Jarvey made a wrong turn and saw a dead end ahead. He groaned in frustration—and the dim lights began to flicker and fade. Not again! He hurried back the way he had come. Something soft brushed his forehead, maybe a cobweb. Tiny legs crept across his cheek, and in revulsion, he swiped at his face. "Stop it!"

The lights steadied, and then he heard what sounded like a party downstairs, with people singing off-key and lots of laughter. The noise led him to the stairway, and at the bottom of the stair he saw Mrs. Macauley leaning on her counter, chatting with a knotty, bent, red-faced man whose nose looked like a potato. She noticed Jarvey and turned toward him with her big-toothed smile. "Hello, then! Had a good nap, have we, love?"

"Uh, fine," Jarvey said with a shrug. "Do you know where my mom and dad are?"

"Went out on that will business, I think, around teatime. Oh, that would be about four o'clock. A man called round for them. Hang on, though—I think your dad left a note for you." She rummaged in the cubbyhole and held out a folded scrap of yellow paper.

Jarvey unfolded it. It was his dad's scrawly handwriting, all right:

> Dear Son,
> Well, we've had a surprise!
> Turns out there's another Midion
> relative who's also mentioned in

old Thaddeus's will, and he's
invited your mom and me to
his home near London for a
brief meeting. He tells me that
Thaddeus died at the ripe
old age of 104—imagine that!
Anyway, we should be back to
the hotel by eight, so if you
wake up before then, ask
Mrs. Macauley to arrange
dinner for you. See you at
eight, if you're awake by then!

The note was signed *Dad.* Jarvey looked up from
the paper. "He says he went to meet another Midion," he began.

The potato-nosed man gasped. It sounded like
a cross between a wheeze and a cough. "Midion?
Midion? Did he say Midion?" His voice was high-
pitched and screechy.

"Sammy," Mrs. Macauley said in a warning tone.

The crooked old man squinted at Jarvey. "You one of them, then?"

"One of what?" Jarvey asked, bewildered.

"One of them wizards, that's what!" Sammy snapped. "One of them Midions, as meddles with powers they shouldn't!"

"Sammy!" Mrs. Macauley's voice cracked like a whip. "This young man is from America. He doesn't know anything about——that."

"He's got the look of them, though," Sammy said, and then to Jarvey's surprise the man began to chant:

> *"Hair like rusty gold, eyes a midnight blue,*
> *Face thin and pale: long, thin fingers too,*
> *Steps quick and strong, but softer than breath,*
> *Heart cold as ice and a soul cold as death!"*

"Sammy Crippen, you've had a pint too much!" Mrs. Macauley scolded. "Along home with you now, and don't worry this poor boy any longer with your silly superstitions!"

Sammy's face clenched in a grim, disapproving expression, and he headed for the door. He paused for a moment, looked back at Jarvey, pointed a bony finger, and said, "Soul cold as death!" Then he was outside, walking away briskly.

"What's . . . what's wrong with him?" Jarvey asked in a shaky voice.

"Just a drop too much of good brown ale," Mrs. Macauley muttered. "Look, though, I might as well tell you the way of it. This part of London is named Hag's Court because of one of your ancestors, Agnes Midion. Back in the days of old Oliver Cromwell, they took Agnes prisoner and executed her as a witch—hanged her on the green just behind this very house, so they say. Her father, Septimus, pleaded with them to spare his daughter's life, but those old Puritans were sure she was a witch and so, well, they killed her. They do say that after she died, not a blade of grass ever grew again on what came to be called the hag's ground. Over time, this part of town began to be known as Hag's Court, in her memory, like. Oh, I know it sounds crazy, but, well, people here have long memories. Are you hungry, then?"

Jarvey was, though his stomach had a strange feeling in it, crawly and wriggly, as if he'd swallowed a handful of squirming live bugs and they weren't happy about the experience. "I could eat something."

"Fish and chips? Local treat!"

Jarvey's mouth watered. "Sounds good."

"Hang about, and I'll have you a tray ready. You can take it back up to your room if you'd like your privacy. Oh, what to drink? Lemonade? It's fizzy here, you know. Yanks always are surprised by that. Or how about a Coke?"

"Coke's fine."

A straight chair, like the one in his room, stood

tucked into a little niche. Jarvey sat on that and leafed through a bewildering English newspaper for a few minutes while Mrs. Macauley disappeared through a pair of double doors into the pub. Jarvey tried to make sense out of a column on cricket, wondering what "bowling a googly" meant.

"Here we are, then."

Jarvey glanced up. Mrs. Macauley was back at the counter, holding a shallow wooden tray holding a plate with crisp-looking golden fish and—french fries! Maybe they were out of chips. "Thanks," Jarvey said. He carried the tray up the stairs and settled down in his room with the tray across his knees. He took a sip of Coke. It was warm. Didn't they know about ice in London? Maybe they had lost the recipe.

The fish was very tasty and the "chips" were good too, better than the fast-food french fries back home. Jarvey wolfed the food down, finished off the tepid soda, and let out a satisfying burp.

After washing the grease from his hands in the little bathroom, Jarvey went into his parents' room to watch TV. The small set could get only five channels, and one of them seemed to be in French. He sat on the edge of the bed and watched a comedy for a while—at least the sound track had a laughing audience on it—but the accents of the actors were hard to understand.

Eight o'clock passed, with no sign of his parents. "They're going to owe me big for this," Jarvey said aloud. He was beginning to feel nervous.

Someone rapped twice, sharply, on the door, and Jarvey jumped right off the bed. His throat felt as if he'd swallowed a rubber ball. "Who is it?" he said, trying to make his voice deep.

The doorknob creaked, then turned, and the door opened, swinging slowly outward. In the growing opening, Jarvey glimpsed a hunched-over, skinny, shadowy figure. Light from the room fell on lank gray hair, and under that a wizened, ratty face, the face of a gaunt man whose burning dark blue eyes bored right into Jarvey's.

"Who are you?" Jarvey squeaked.

The man didn't answer for a second. Then, in a raspy, hoarse voice, he growled, "You're a Midion, all right. Hair like rusty gold. Eyes midnight blue. I've come to warn you, boy, you and your father and your mother. Heed me! You're all in danger. Beware the book!" His hand, a pale, crooked claw, scrabbled at the door for a moment and then swung it shut with a bang. He was gone, leaving Jarvey feeling dazed, his heart pounding.

Jarvey came out of his stunned trance as if he had just felt an electric shock. "Wait!" Jarvey was at the door in two steps, and he had it open at once. He stood frozen in the doorway, staring out into the empty corridor.

It was impossible. The man couldn't have vanished that fast.

But vanished he had, as if he had dissolved into the dark, musty air in the hallway.

CHAPTER 2

Message by Night

Jarvey closed the door and leaned against the wall, feeling his heart thudding hard inside his chest, as though he had just completed a hard sprint. He told himself to be cool, but then a shrill warbling sound made him jump as if he had just touched a live electric wire. With a gasp of relief, he realized the noise was just the telephone beside his parents' bed.

Jarvey got to it as it rang a second time. For a moment he paused with his hand on the receiver. To calm himself, he took a deep, deliberate breath, swallowed his apprehension, and answered the phone with a somewhat shaky "H-hello?"

"Son!"

Jarvey breathed out a lungful of air, sudden relief at the sound of the familiar voice making his muscles go limp. "Dad! Where are you? Are you okay? Why—"

"Calm down, now. We're quite well, thank you very much. However, we want you to see this fantastic place," his father's voice said. "You'll love it. Now, I know it's a little late. You needn't worry about it. We'll move back to the hotel tomorrow, after the will business is taken care of, but you really have to see this wonderful Midion mansion. Get ready—your great-uncle and his driver are already on the way to pick you up."

"But Dad—"

"I need you to pack some clothing for tomorrow and your night things. Your great-uncle Siyamon will—"

"What? Simon?"

"Siyamon! He does not like to be called Simon, so be careful, please. It's an old-fashioned name, to be sure, but then, such names rather run in our family, I daresay." Then, with a click, the line went dead, and Jarvey was left with a strange metallic taste in his mouth and a creeping suspicion in his mind. The voice was his father's, but Dr. Midion *never* used phrases like "to be sure" or "I daresay." He had sounded so strange, not like himself at all—

The TV sound suddenly blared so loud, it made him jump. He scrambled to the set and turned it down, switched it off. The volume knob had been turned all the way, though he hadn't touched it.

Jarvey took long, deep breaths, telling himself there are no such things as magic or wizards—or even Spriggans. Calm down. Someone's coming to take you to your parents.

Jarvey didn't have to do much to get ready, just throw a change of clothes, his toothbrush, and his pajamas into his suitcase. That took about five minutes. For the next half hour he sat tensely on the edge of his parents' bed, waiting.

And then a knock sounded, a light triple knock at the door, tap-tap-tap, so soft that it was hard to tell whether he had heard it or imagined it. Jarvey raced to the door and opened it.

He found himself standing face-to-face with a shriveled old man. As a younger fellow, the stranger might have stood over six feet tall, but it was hard to tell because now his shoulders stooped badly, and his long neck stretched out like a tortoise's. Shadowed hollows lay in his lean face, darkest beneath his sharp cheekbones. His deep-set blue eyes peered from under craggy, shaggy white eyebrows, and long white hair curled down around his ears and onto his shoulders.

The newcomer leaned on a silver-headed cane, and his thin, wrinkled lips wore a sharp, dangerous smile. "Ah," the man purred. "My great-grand-nephew Jarvis. Allow me to introduce myself. I am Siyamon Midion. My driver is waiting. Come along, my good young lad. We are in rather a hurry." As he spoke, his head swayed gently back and forth on his long, creased neck.

"Where are Mom and Dad?" Jarvey asked.

"Why, resting very comfortably, I daresay, at my home, Bywater House." The man's silky voice sounded like the rumble of a contented cat. He chuckled, a low, liquid sound. "We name our houses on this side of the Atlantic, you know. Bywater House belonged to my great-great grandfather many years ago, and now it belongs to me. Is that your bag? Bring it along." He held out his hand, his bony finger pointing to Jarvey's small suitcase.

"I, uh, don't have the key to lock the door——"

"Not to worry," Siyamon said. "All is in order." He flicked his hand, and as if he had done a magic trick, a brass key gleamed in his thin fingers. "Your father gave me this and asked me to lock up."

Jarvey relaxed a little. Siyamon could have gotten the key only from his dad, so he must be all right. He picked up his suitcase and stepped out into the gloomy hall, and Siyamon closed and locked the door, the bolt clicking home with a final, surprisingly loud sound.

Neither of them spoke as they made their way through the narrow corridor. The little tulip-shaped bulbs did not flicker as they passed. Siyamon led the way down the stair. In the little nook of a lobby, Siyamon reached to seize Jarvey's left arm above the elbow and hurried him out, with the suitcase banging painfully against the boy's right knee.

Outside, a long black car sat parked beneath a streetlamp. In the deepening gloom of twilight, Jarvey stared at the car, a limousine, a midnight-colored Rolls-Royce with a protruding hood and a long, curved trunk. Its engine murmured softly, sending a thin gray plume of exhaust vapor curling out into the evening air. Beside the car stood a uniformed driver. He took Jarvey's suitcase and opened the back door.

"Quickly now, lad, get in, get in," Siyamon urged.

Jarvey climbed in, then sank into the deep backseat. The interior of the car held a scent of mildly sweet spices, like cinnamon and nutmeg combined. The driver put the car in gear and with a lurch it leaped out onto the street and turned hard right. Jarvey fumbled for seat belts, but the big car didn't have them. He looked out the window and realized that it was so heavily tinted that he could see only the passing pale blurs of streetlamps. Although he could tell they took a good many curves at a pretty high speed, Jarvey had no sense of where they were heading.

"Soon we shall be there," Siyamon said softly. "It is not so very far. We will arrive before you know it, Jarvis." He held his cane in the middle and stared at the silver handle. "I find your parents quite charming, dear boy. They feel you will enjoy a tour of my home, perhaps tomorrow, as they and I are attending the reading of the will. I shall have my driver and man of all work, Mr. Rupert Henge, show you about."

Jarvey gave a neutral grunt that conveyed neither agreement nor disagreement. Siyamon Midion hummed a monotonous, repetitive little tune and continued to hold his cane out in front of him, slowly rotating it so the silver handle made a complete circle about once every minute. Jarvey stared dully at it. It caught reflections from the faint light coming through the windshield, and the gleams blurred in his vision, becoming random sparkles of white light against the blackness of night. Jarvey's breath slowed, his eyelids drooped, and in spite of his long sleep earlier that day, he began to nod off.

"What?" he asked suddenly. It seemed to him that Siyamon had just asked him something very strange.

"Do you have the art?" the old man repeated softly.

"I—I don't know about art," he said. "Maybe my dad—he teaches history—"

"He has no art, however," Siyamon purred. "His

grandmother ran away from home, you see, when his father was only an infant. She ran to America, it appears, and with her child, she hid there from her husband and his family. And your grandfather was raised without knowing of his heritage. He raised his own son that way, and he his son, as *ordinary* people. The art develops only if it appears early and the possessor then trains. Pity not to know the Midion art. Why, a Midion without art might just as well not exist at all." The cane glittered in deep darkness, and Jarvey dozed again.

Then, somehow, Jarvey found himself outside the car and standing in a doorway. He had no memory of getting out of the limousine. A weight, as light as a landing sparrow, touched his right shoulder, and he realized that old Siyamon had placed his bony hand there. "I have a comfortable room prepared for you," he said in his whispery, rustley voice. "First, though, I know you would like to visit my library. Your parents couldn't tear themselves away from what I have there. Yes, they found themselves literally enchanted in the library."

Jarvey was too tired to reply, and with a light pressure of his hand on the boy's shoulder, Siyamon steered Jarvey down a dark, walnut-paneled corridor with a high, curved ceiling. They passed half a dozen closed doors. Jarvey couldn't hear a sound apart from their footfalls on what seemed to be a bare wood floor. An open stone archway at the end of the hall led into a high-ceilinged room illuminated by four tall floor lamps, each with a heavy parchment shade. Each one gave about as much light as a birthday candle. Jarvey's head felt floaty and strange. He vaguely grasped that the room was huge, the walls stretching up for twelve or fifteen feet, all lined with row after row of floor-to-ceiling bookshelves, every shelf crammed with ancient volumes. The dusty, spicy scent of old books filled his nostrils.

"Here we are. Very good, my lad. Just walk

straight ahead," suggested Siyamon. "Please take just a moment to examine the book on the stand. It is a family heirloom. You want to open it, don't you?"

Jarvey couldn't answer, though he did feel a growing desire to do as Siyamon suggested. His feet dragged him forward, to an oak book stand that bore a single volume, a tall, narrow book. Its cover was a pebbled leather the color of old dried blood, with gleaming brass hinges on the spine and a brass catch holding the book closed.

Standing on an intensely dark blue carpet, Jarvey's very toes tingled. A circle, seemingly drawn in liquid moonlight, shimmered around the book stand. Within its perimeter glimmered the silvery letters of some unknown alphabet, forming words that spun slowly counterclockwise within the circle. Jarvey hesitated at the edge of this boundary.

"Don't be alarmed," Siyamon said behind him, his voice strange and sharp. "A Midion should not fear the circle. It keeps out only unwanted intruders, not members of our own family. Go ahead, my boy. Open the book and read. We have held its dark secrets for more than five hundred years, the Grimoire of the Midions. It is time to claim your birthright, my fine young fellow."

Grimoire? The word echoed nonsensically in Jarvey's mind, fading to tinny whispers. He felt chilled, shivering uncontrollably. He dragged his feet over the edge of the circle, feeling as he had in his dream, as though his legs had turned to lead.

His hands floated at an impossible distance from him, bloodless spiders at the end of mere wisps of arms. The orange glow of the lamp flooded over them as they touched the cover of that strange book. The light gave his hands no color. As if they knew by themselves what they needed to do, Jarvey's fingers found the latch that released the clasp. It felt burning cold, and Jarvey winced as he touched it, but with an effort he flicked the complicated release back and then flipped open the clasp.

Beware the book.

Where had that come from?

Siyamon was circling him, prowling the edge of the glowing circle. "The last chapter. Open to the final page, my good nephew. The final page."

Beware the book.

Where did the warning come from? Jarvey told himself he had to be dreaming, that this was another nightmare, and he tried to force himself to wake up. He saw his pale and distant hands, the left one gripping the edge of the book stand, the right poised to open the Grimoire.

With every ounce of his will, Jarvey drew his hands back, gasping for breath. "No," he groaned, his voice thin and weak. "No, I don't want to."

The four dim lamps flared into momentary, blinding light, as if touched by lightning, then faded again.

Siyamon's breath hissed. "No art? You do have a touch of it then, eh? But wild art, untamed, and you don't know how to use it. Fool of a boy!" The old man had circled all the way around and now stood across from Jarvey, his toes at the very edge of the shimmering circle. He rapped his cane on the floor, the deep carpet muffling its sound.

Jarvey felt a rumble, a lurching, rolling heave, and thought wildly that he was experiencing an earthquake. He tried to back away from the book.

Old Siyamon's lips writhed, and his face became a mask of anger. "If you will not open the book, I shall open it for you!" He pointed his cane across the circle and roared, *"Abrire ultimas!"*

The book's cover slammed back, and the pages fluttered as though a hurricane wind were ripping at them. Jarvey saw page after page flash by, all thickly covered with handwriting in bloodred ink. The handwriting changed as the pages flipped past, now looping and heavy, now spiked and thin, as though many hands had taken turns at writing the book over the years. Faraway screeches, screams, groans burst from the flying pages, and Jarvey fought against the weird sensation that the book was pulling him forward, like a powerful magnet.

His stomach heaved as Jarvey felt his body dissolving, flowing, being pulled toward the book, swirling like water gurgling down a drain. He opened his mouth to shout and felt the air being drawn from his lungs—

A third person burst into the room, over to Jarvey's left. "The book! I warned you! It is drawing you in! Turn away, grab something, quickly!"

Siyamon Midion spun toward the figure, snarling a curse, and Jarvey's mind cleared momentarily.

Reaching out, Jarvey seized the book with both hands, stopping its pages from turning. He held on, one hand clutching the front cover and about half the pages, the other holding the back cover and the other pages. Beneath his hands the book actually moved, writhing like an angry animal.

Lightning crackled outside the circle, red and blue. The air sizzled, reeking of sulfur and burning cloth. The book grew harder to handle, bucking and heaving in Jarvey's hands, trying to break free of his grip. Jarvey held it in a death grip as he recognized the gray-haired, rat-faced man who had told him to beware the book—the book! And now—

Both men were shrieking foreign words, red lighting flashing from the tip of Siyamon's cane and blue lightning leaping from the stranger's outstretched fingertips, and the very air crackled with their fury. The book felt as if it were expanding in Jarvey's grasp—

His body jerked, flowing forward, pulled by a physical attraction he could not overcome. As he fell, his arms wrenched behind him, as if the book had passed right through his body—or his body had passed through the book.

Then . . . Jarvey felt whole again, solid, himself but in darkness, free-falling, the book clutched tight

39

against his chest. He tumbled, head up, feet up, into whistling, freezing air, into endless night.

A moment later or a hundred years before, he crashed to earth with an impact that blew out his consciousness like a candle flame caught in a tornado.

CHAPTER 3
Into the Fog

Slowly, feeling returned. Jarvey's first thought was that he must have been hit with a fastball, because his head throbbed so painfully. Jarvey's left arm, twisted beneath his body, tingled with pins-and-needles numbness. His fingers ached as if they had been broken, and he gradually became aware that he still clutched the book.

Lost in total darkness, Jarvey sat up with a lurch of effort. From somewhere far away he heard a low murmur of voices, but he could make out no distinct words. Feeling around in the dark, he thumped his hand against a sharp corner. He swept his palm over wood and discovered he was sitting on a hard floor beside some kind of desk or table.

With difficulty, Jarvey hauled himself up, swaying on his feet. His left hand still held the book. His mouth and throat felt as dry as the Sahara. "Hey," he croaked, but the darkness swallowed the weak sound. He stretched out his right hand and inched across the floor until he reached what felt like a shelf of close-packed books.

Still in Siyamon's library, then. What had happened to the lamps? Edging his way to the right, Jarvey reached a door. He felt around, found the handle, and turned it, opening the door to dim yellow light. Before him the arched hall led away, illuminated only by four fat candles flickering wanly in wall sconces. Halfway down the hall on the right a door stood ajar, and the murmuring voices were coming from there.

"Not you, of course," a querulous old man was saying. "None of my trusted advisors. But the rest, I tell you, must go back. We cannot tolerate so many idle hands, so many immortal mouths to feed!"

42

"Sir," another voice said, "with respect, that cannot be done. The spell would require tremendous power, and it would leave you dangerously weak."

"Do you dare question me?" the first voice thundered.

Jarvey crept down the hall, close enough to peek in through the partly opened door. He could glimpse men sitting at a long table, oddly dressed in long black double-breasted coats. They looked like figures in a historical movie, long sideburns on their cheeks, high collars, old-fashioned ties. Three of them were sitting at the near end of the table.

One glanced up, caught sight of Jarvey, and sprang to his feet. "My lord, if I might be excused. I have a slight indisposition."

"Go, go," the old man said in his grumbling voice. He was out of sight, toward the right end of the table. "Now, Dodson, as to the question of the power it would require . . ."

The man who had risen stepped into the hall and

closed the door, cutting off the voice. "You are asking for trouble," he said sternly. "To interrupt the Inner Council is a gross violation of propriety."

"I've got to find my mom and dad," Jarvey blurted, his voice trembling with fear.

"Hush!" The man gripped his arm, spun him around, and marched him down the hall. At the far end, he opened a door. He reached up, took a candle from its sconce, and pushed Jarvey inside a small parlor with a scatter of small tables and chairs, each table holding a candelabra. The man lit one of these from the candle he held. "Who are you? Kitchen boy?"

"I'm Jarvey Midion," Jarvey began.

The man dropped the candle he held, and it went out with a splash of melted wax. "The devil you are! Another one?" He took a step forward, narrowing his eyes. "Hair like—"

"Don't say it!" Jarvey said. "Look, I have the Grimoire. Siyamon Midion—"

The man bent forward. "That can't be—not the Grimoire? Here? Impossible!"

Jarvey grated his teeth. "I want to find my mom and dad!" he snapped.

The candelabra shivered on its table, doing an eccentric little dance, the flames flickering. The man grabbed it. "The Grimoire here," he repeated. "What year is it? Tell me quickly."

"It—it's 2006," Jarvey stammered, bewildered.

The man groaned, sinking into a chair. "Then the Curse of the Midions endures into two more centuries! The book, the cursed book!"

Jarvey's eyes flew wide. "I know you! You looked a lot older, but you warned me. You said to beware the book, and I saw you fighting Siyamon with some kind of magic—"

"Quiet," the man said. "I have no time to explain now. Jarvey—that is your name, you said?—you are in grave danger. That book is deadly here. It could cause—well, it could cause the world to end."

"What?"

"Shh! Not so loud! Listen, I am—well, call me a cousin, and that won't be far wrong. You must trust me. Keep that book safe, keep it out of Tantalus Midion's hands at all costs, do you hear? You have come directly to his house, to Bywater—"

"It's Siyamon's house," Jarvey said.

"It may be in your world. This is not your world, do you understand? This is not your world, not your year, not your past. This is all a fiction, a dream made real by Tantalus Midion, as his ancestors used the Grimoire to make their own evil dreams real and then went to inhabit them. You, I, all of this around us—we are inside the book you hold!"

"I don't understand you!" Jarvey shouted. One of the candles drooped and ran, liquid dripping over the man's hand. It left a long stalactite of wax, but he did not seem to notice it.

"We must get you out of this," he said, setting

46

the candelabra down. "Call me Zoroaster. You must trust me. I will try to find some safe place for you, but you must not call attention to yourself. Wait here." Zoroaster slipped out the door, pulled it shut behind him, and his footsteps faded. Jarvey slumped into a chair, feeling as if his legs had turned to water. What had happened to his parents?

In a few moments, the door opened again. "Here," Zoroaster said, tossing a cloak to Jarvey. "Wrap this around you, and keep that book under it. You are to follow me and keep still. Don't say a word!"

"I want my mom and dad," Jarvey insisted.

"I—very well, then, I shall try to take you to them. Only do as I say, and quickly! We haven't a moment to lose!"

Jarvey draped the cloak around himself, and Zoroaster fastened it at the throat. "Keep that book hidden, whatever you do. Now, you must follow me. Stay three steps behind me, look down at the floor, and don't speak a word. Let's go."

Jarvey nearly jogged in Zoroaster's wake as the man strode fast out into the hall. They followed the corridor away from the library, stepping out into an enormous room whose ceiling was so high that it lost itself in darkness. A man stepped forward, offering a much longer cloak and a silver-headed cane. "Leaving, my lord?"

Zoroaster threw the cloak around his shoulders. "Yes. This boy brought an urgent message."

The man opened the front door, and Zoroaster led the way out into a damp, fog-wrapped night. In the distance gas lamps flared, but they made only ruddy blurs in the darkness. A long gravel drive crunched beneath Jarvey's feet, and he had the impression that some kind of tall iron fence walled them in on either side. Ahead of him, Zoroaster called, "Open, there!"

Someone in the fog responded, "Yes, my lord," and a heavy iron gate groaned on its hinges. They stepped out through a gap between two small structures—guardhouses, Jarvey realized, like the ones his dad had shown him in a brochure about London.

Zoroaster stooped and said, "Into the carriage, boy. I have some questions."

A black horse-drawn carriage loomed in the darkness. Jarvey had trouble finding the narrow steps, but with an impatient boost from Zoroaster he half-stumbled inside, collapsing on a seat. The man clambered in, sat opposite him, and closed the door. He thumped the ceiling with his cane, and with a clatter and rattle, the carriage jerked into motion.

"Where are my parents?" Jarvey demanded. "Siyamon took them into his house."

Zoroaster, visible only as a silhouette in the darkness, said, "Listen to me, Jarvey Midion. The house I have taken you from is not the Bywater of the real world, of your world. Please understand, this whole city is the creation of a great sorcerer. Tantalus Midion is master here, and I daresay he is the great-grandfather of the Siyamon Midion in your world. He was married, years ago, though his wife died. His son he left behind when he used the Grimoire to open the gateway to this place."

"You keep saying crazy things," Jarvey accused.

"I know they sound insane to you. Try to understand, though. The Grimoire is filled with magic secrets. It allows the Midions to escape death in the real world, to write spells of great complexity that open other worlds to them. These worlds are—are shapeless, unformed, until the spells are written, and then they become real. The Grimoire that you have somehow brought here—well, think of it as containing Tantalus's world, and many other worlds besides. That is not wholly true, but it may give you an idea of how important the Grimoire is. It was first created in the year 1659 by Septimus Midion, who resented the death of his innocent daughter. He wanted to create a world of dreams where his daughter still lived, you understand, and he vanished inside the book, leaving—well, leaving his son, who was as confused as you must be."

"How can a person vanish in a book?" Jarvey asked.

"A Midion could," Zoroaster said darkly. "They were a numerous family at that time, and many of them were gifted with the art of magic. Later Midions came into possession of the Grimoire, and they twisted it and misused its magic—or perhaps it twisted them. The book gives such great power that it tempts a sorcerer to evil."

Jarvey was shaking his head. "This is all crazy. Look, I just want to go home! You said you'd take me to find Mom and Dad."

The coach had been rattling along, but as Jarvey spoke, it slowed and halted. With a snarl of anger, Zoroaster opened the coach door and leaned out into the fog. "Driver!"

"Sorry, my lord. Curfew wagon is coming. They'll want to see our papers."

A dim light shone through the open door. Zoroaster hissed between his teeth, then threw the door open. In a whisper, he ordered, "Get out and hide! Here, take this." He waved a shadowy hand, and Jarvey, reaching out, felt a card being thrust into his grip. "That is my home address. Come to see me tomorrow, as quickly as you can. Come by day! I will help you if I can."

"My dad—"

"Your parents are not here! I lied to get you out of Bywater House! Get out now, or you'll be captured." Zoroaster seized Jarvey's arm and practically hurled him out of the coach. The cloak ripped away, and Jarvey stumbled into a dark opening, an alley between two indistinct brick buildings. He could hear the slow clopping of horses, the trundle of wheels. A hand bell rang.

The driver of the coach snapped a whip, and the carriage rumbled off into the fog. The bell clanged again, and from the darkness came a rough voice: "Twelve o'clock of a foul night, and ye be warned!"

Jarvey heard another sound, a sharp hiss, almost a whistle, from the dark alley behind him. "Is anybody there?"

In response, a quick, stealthy, skittering sound came from the alley. Rats, maybe. Jarvey gripped the book, wondering if it was heavy enough to clobber a rat.

"Woss that?" The sharp voice came from down the street, from the direction of the wagon rumble. "You hear that, Georgie?"

"Nar, ya got fog in yer lug-holes," an older man's voice snapped. "On wiv it, Bert, and less of yer lip."

And now a dark bulk loomed out of the fog, a heavy wagon, pulled by a single plodding horse. Jarvey opened his mouth to yell—

"Mmpff!" A hand clamped over his open mouth, and other hands seized his arms. He felt himself being dragged away from the street, away from the streetlamp. Breath whistled in someone's nostrils, two or three people, by the sound of it. An urgent whisper said, "In here, quick!"

The hand over his mouth didn't move, but the figures hauling at him broke away. They pushed at him from behind, and Jarvey stumbled deeper into the narrow alley. The trundling sound of the wheels and the clopping of the horse's hooves stopped and he desperately tried to wrench free and yell for help.

"Sst!" The voice was right in his ear, and the warm breath smelled of onions. "Quiet, boy! You want the Mill Press to get you?"

The grumbling older man's voice came from the fog: "Nuffin' there, I tells ya. You ain't gonna please Nibs by prowlin' around lookin' for runagates what ain't there."

The younger man's voice, higher pitched and quarrelsome, came back: "I heard somethin', I tells ya."

"Rats, or a mangy stray dog. Get on with yer, Bert. Some of us has homes ter go to, an' th' mills is hungry fer yon bearns. If you makes us late, on yer head be it!"

Bert growled a curse, but Jarvey heard the crack of a whip, and a moment later the wagon rolled away. He wasn't sure, but he thought he heard another sound, softer than the horse or the men, and unsettling. Children were crying somewhere, maybe in the back of the wagon.

The hands didn't release Jarvey until the wagon had passed out of earshot. Then the person whose hand had clapped his mouth shut finally let go and said, "Well, cully, you're a green 'un and no mistake. Run away, have we? Come to join the Dodgers, have we? Rich boy out for adventure, I'll wager."

"You're a girl," Jarvey said, surprised.

Someone giggled, and the girl snapped, "None of that, Carks. Let's get this baby to the snug, and then we'll see what's what. Maybe he's got some brass in his pockets to pay us for his rescue."

"Rescue? What do you mean? Look, I'm an American, and I have to get to a police station—"

"Walk-er!" one of the shadows said, then burst into a giggling fit. "Go to a tippers' station? You've got rocks in your nog, is what! Same as trotting to the mills, it is, and shoutin' 'Oi! Here, take me!' Tippers' station! Find yourself chained to a loom in about half a shake, you do that."

"I was kidnapped," Jarvey said desperately. "A man who said he was my uncle took me to, well, he said it was Bywater House, and he and—"

A hand slapped his face, so hard that Jarvey saw an explosion of yellow. "Nibs took you, did he?" the girl growled. "Well, you'll not be telling him of the likes of us, else you're fish food tonight, sharps."

"Ow," Jarvey said, rubbing his cheek. Then he realized he had dropped the Midion Grimoire. "Where's my book?"

"Got it here, cully," another boy said. "Here,

reach out. Where are you? Here it is, take it. Can't none of us read, no gates."

The sharp corner of the book poked into Jarvey's chest, and he took it from the boy, feeling its weight almost with gratitude.

"Come on," the girl said. "Mill Press will have runners out."

They shoved him, led him, and grumbled at his slowness as they made their way through a maze of alleys and byways, under bridges beside a river that reeked of stagnant mud and dead fish, through open windows and into basements crowded with stacks of crates and what seemed to be rusted machinery. "Where are we going?" Jarvey asked three or four times, but he never got an answer. It was like some of his bad dreams, nightmares of endless running, to something or from something, in which he could make no progress.

However, this night's running found an end at last. From ahead of him, Jarvey heard a complicated rapping, answered by another series of taps, and then a dim opening appeared, a door. The kids behind him thrust him forward, down a steep incline, to the doorway, then through, hurriedly, and the shadowy figure of the girl held aside a hanging blanket and urgently beckoned to him. Jarvey ducked under it.

One dripping candle provided a faint light, but to his weary eyes it blazed bright enough to dazzle him. His head ached, and he felt every bruise he had collected. Jarvey had the impression of being in an immense room, something almost the size of a cathedral, but someone—the kids around him, Jarvey supposed—had walled off a portion of it. Splintered wooden crates, stacked more than head-high, made a hollow square about twelve feet on a side. A ragged gray curtain covered the only entrance. More pieces of gray cloth, roughly stitched together, made up a kind of drooping, sagging ceiling overhead.

Jarvey saw four boys and one girl, all of them

staring at him silently. The youngest of them looked about eight years old. He squeaked, "Who've we brought home, then, Betsy?"

"A rum 'un," the girl said with a grin. She was close to Jarvey's age, but incredibly dirty. Her hair might have been red, but it was hard to tell in the candlelight. She, or someone, had hacked it short. Bangs hung on her forehead, but the rest of her hair spiked away in all directions. Her eyes were green, her nose tilted up at the tip, and her mouth wide. Like the others, she wore a shirt and pants too big for her, the pants belted at the waist with a rope, and she was barefoot.

The youngest boy had been waiting in the tent-like enclosure, but the other three had been the ones shoving Jarvey along. One looked as if he might be Pakistani or Indian, with black hair and eyes. The second was a year or two younger than Jarvey, and he had blond hair that fell into a cap of curls. The last was a tall, lanky kid who was probably thirteen or fourteen. He had shaved his head down to stubble, and he was missing two front teeth.

"Lookin's free, cully," Betsy said. "Strange clothes you have there."

"Where are we?" Jarvey asked.

"Call it the Den," Betsy said. "Where we live, when we're not runnin' from the tippers or the pressers. Only you got to pay rent, see? Got any brass on you?"

Jarvey furrowed his brow. "Brass? Money, you mean?"

"American, is that?" the Indian-looking boy said. "Sounds posh, dunnit?"

Jarvey fumbled in his jeans pockets. No money. Nothing. "I don't have any, uh, brass," he said. "Look, if I could get to the police—"

The youngest kid, the one who had let them in, had flung himself on the floor. Now he sprang up, balling his fists. "Go to!" he yelled. "Want the tippers, do yer? What is he, Bets, some bloody spy?"

"Dunno what he is," Betsy said, holding out an arm to keep the boy back. "Talked about the place, though. The one by the river. And he has that book."

The boy stared. "Strike me! That ain't *the* Book, though. Is it?"

"Shut it, Puddler," Betsy said softly. "Let's have some jaw work and see what we can learn. All right, American. Tell us your name to begin with."

"It's Jarvey Midion," he began, "but—"

Something exploded against him, and the next thing Jarvey knew, he lay flat on his back, with two of the boys pulling the youngest, the one Betsy had called Puddler, off him. Heaving for breath, Jarvey realized that the younger kid had plowed right into him, hitting him hard in the stomach. He groaned.

"Manners, Puds," Betsy said, hunkering down close to Jarvey. "True word, American? You one of them? A Midion?"

"That's my name," Jarvey muttered, picking up

the book, which he had dropped. "But people call me Jarvey."

Betsy nodded at the book. "And you use that, do you? You know the art?"

"What do you mean, 'art'? Everyone keeps saying that. I don't know what it means."

"Tell us what you do know," Betsy suggested.

So he told them everything, from the arrival of the letter to his being shoved out of the carriage near the alley. None of them seemed to believe that he had flown over the ocean. One of the boys, the oldest one, tapped his head and rolled his eyes when Jarvey tried to explain the airplane trip.

When he had finished, Betsy looked troubled. "You lot, scarper till I call," she said, and without a word, the boys left the improvised room, ducking one by one through the blanket-hung opening.

As soon as they were alone, Betsy sat beside Jarvey, who had pulled himself up to a sitting position, his back against a stack of crates. She said, "Look in my eyes, Jarvey."

His own eyes felt hot with tears ready to begin, but he defiantly looked into Betsy's green gaze.

She stared deep into him. "Right," she said. "Now, the question. Do you or do you not have the art?"

"I don't know what you mean," Jarvey said.

Her lips barely moved. "Magic. Sorcery. The High Art. Can you do it or no?"

Jarvey snorted. "No, I can't. There's no such thing."

Her eyes bored into him. "You sure of that?"

A window shattering. Overhead lights blazing too bright, then exploding in sparks. A baseball bat blowing itself to pieces.

"I'm not sure of anything," Jarvey said at last. "But I can't *do* magic, if that's what you mean. Stuff sometimes just sort of happens, that's all."

"So you can't do magic, but you flew through the air, across the wide ocean."

"Sure, on an airplane," Jarvey said. "A jet? An airliner?"

She shook her head. "Never heard of such."

Jarvey groaned. "Where's Hag's Court?" he asked.

"Never heard of that, neither."

"It's not far from Kensington. Look, this is London, isn't it?"

To his surprise, Betsy's eyes glistened as if she were about to weep. "Nah, cully, wrong there. This ain't London Town. This here's Lunnon, and Nibs—that's Tantalus Midion, and I reckon he's a relative of yours—made it with his art."

"That's what someone else told me. It doesn't make sense."

"Nah, not by night tide, I s'pose not." Betsy took a deep, thoughtful breath. "I can't make you out at all, cully. You tell the truth, but your truth is cracked and crazy. Any gate, we saved your skin from the Mill Press. And if that is the right, true Grimoire, then you might be of use to us after all."

"Here," Jarvey said, holding out the book. "If you want this, take it and call it my rent—"

Quick as a snake, Betsy pulled herself away from him. "Nah! Don't hold that thing towards me! If it is what you say it is, I wouldn't touch it for a thousand pound! They do say that whenever that thing opens in front of people, it transports them away."

"T-transports them?"

"Grabs 'em body and soul, and pulls them from their life and their world into somethin' else. That book's a work of art, it is, and I've heard older people say that none but a Midion can use it." Betsy crouched. "You keep it, but don't try to open it. Not for your life. You'd best grab yourself a corner and sleep if you can. Look, don't try to get away, see? We sleeps light, and we don't rightways trust you yet."

She whistled, and a moment later the four boys came back in. Without looking away from Jarvey, Betsy said, "Right, then. He's true story, so far as he knows, and he's Artless. No brass on him, but he bears the Midion name, and that might just be worth somethin' to somebody. All sleep now, and in the morning we'll sort it out."

Jarvey didn't have to do much to get ready for bed. The oldest boy, whose name seemed to be Plum, showed him where the toilet was. It wasn't much, just a trough of running water, but Jarvey wasn't picky by that time. He did see that they were in a vast basement room, with ancient, cobweb-strung beams high overhead and crumbling brick walls all around.

They went back to the improvised room, where the other three boys were already snoring. Betsy sat brooding in the corner closest to the curtain-hung doorway. Jarvey hesitated beside her, then said, "Look, I'm kind of hungry."

"You too, cully?" She gave him a fierce grin. "We're all sharp set. Bed now, over there." She jerked her head toward a kind of pad in the corner, made up of odds and ends of carpet and fabric. "We'll see about getting vittles for you in the morning, if we decide you're to be let live. Go on, go on, bed now."

Jarvey knelt and arranged the carpet ends and bundles of cloth as well as he could. He stretched out on it. Across the room, Betsy blew out the candle, and darkness flooded in.

Jarvey turned this way and that, squirming, trying to make himself comfortable and reasonably warm. He dragged some of the rough cloth over himself as a makeshift blanket. His bruises and scrapes twinged dismally. All around him, the other kids snored, coughed, muttered in their dreams. Jarvey's neck began to cramp.

After a few minutes, Jarvey sat up in his improvised bed and wrapped the book in some scraps of cloth. He slipped it under his head. It was a hard pillow, but by that time exhaustion had caught up, and he was past caring. Right now, he would give anything to return to that dreary hotel with his mom and dad. Confused, worn out, and more than a little afraid, Jarvey did the impossible: He fell asleep.

CHAPTER 4
The Cold Light of Day

From the depths of sleep Jarvey surfaced suddenly, thrashing and yelling. He opened his eyes and saw the crate-walled room in a thin gray light. He was alone. As he scrambled up, he remembered the book and unwrapped it. The hanging blanket that served as the door had been twitched aside, and a little light seeped through the opening.

He peeked out. The cavernous basement had a few high, small windows, and through these, dusty bars of daylight slanted in, buttresses against the dark wall. Jarvey could see nothing through the windows. They were fifteen feet above the floor, and their panes had been so bleared with grime that they were barely translucent.

The room stretched out for a hundred feet or more, and fifty feet from side to side. A double row of pillars helped to support the raftered ceiling. Six huge panels, heavily outlined in two-foot-thick timbers, looked like trapdoors that opened up to a floor somewhere above. Dust lay thick everywhere, and scuttling spiders had strung their webs over the bricks and every other surface. Corroded gear wheels the size of dinner plates littered the stone floor, and a few broken-down machines, bigger than automobiles, crouched against the far wall, some upright, some on their sides.

Where had everyone gone? Jarvey wandered until he found a single splintered door. It was unlocked, and it creaked open on rusty hinges when Jarvey tried it. A steep ramp led up into what looked like an alley, narrow and dark between featureless walls of sooty brick.

Jarvey fished in his pocket until he found the crumpled card that Zoroaster had forced on him.

Did the man really know where his mom and dad might be? Zoroaster had admitted lying to him, but he seemed to be Jarvey's only hope. Jarvey studied the engraved script on the card: Lord P. Zoroaster, Ruling Council. Beneath that was what had to be an address: 3, Royal Crescent.

Stuffing the card back into his pocket, Jarvey crept up the incline, holding the book tight. The alley was narrow, only about three feet side to side. To his right, it ran for fifty feet and then bent around the corner of the huge building and vanished in darkness. To his left he saw light. When he reached the alley mouth, Jarvey paused, his jaw dropping.

Early-morning light made a cloudy sky milky-white. A ghastly throng of men, women, and children trudged past in the street, all of them wearing coarse, ragged gray clothing, most barefoot. Their heads drooped, and they all looked hopeless, helpless. In the washed-out light of morning, the soot-streaked buildings loomed like forbidding prison walls. A few heavyset, tough-looking men in black strode beside the crowd, brandishing six-foot-long staves. Now and then one of them yelled and struck out at a straggler, who would cower, cry out, or stumble.

Jarvey shrank back into the shadows. One of the guards jerked his head around, his eyes narrowing. Jarvey backed away as the man shouted to one of the other guards and then came toward him, brandishing his heavy staff.

Looking wildly around, Jarvey realized he had no choice—he had already retreated past the entrance to the basement. He hurried through the alley, away from the street and the man, took a sharp left turn and found himself in a dead-end passage between two crumbling brick walls, a passage no more than a yard wide.

Trapped! Jarvey whirled, but already he heard the crunch of the man's boots out in the main alley. He'd be caught, forced into that line of hopeless people—

Tucking the book inside his shirt again, Jarvey looked around frantically. Suddenly an idea struck him. He braced his back against the right wall and pressed his feet against the left one. He walked a little way up the wall, holding himself there by the pressure of his back, and then hitched himself up. Back and forth, first moving his feet, then his back, he crept up until he was a good twelve feet or more above the ground.

Then he froze. The man with the staff had reached the mouth of his dark, narrow passage. Jarvey tried to force his heartbeat to slow and held his breath. The leather-clad man leaned in and peered down the blind alley to the far end. He sniffed, like a bloodhound.

His muscles trembling, Jarvey thought desperately: *Don't see me! Don't see me!*

The guard looked up.

Jarvey swallowed. He would be taken, and the guard would find the Grimoire—

The guard below continued to sweep his gaze up, past Jarvey. And then he turned on his heel and walked away, his footsteps echoing and fading as he strode back toward the street.

Jarvey felt as if he would fall. How could the guard have missed him? He had looked straight at Jarvey, but had seemed to look through him.

Climbing down was much worse than climbing up had been. Jarvey stared at his sneakers as he inched down, and in the darkness he saw something strange: Sparks danced around the toes of his shoes as he took baby steps downward, silvery white sparks like tiny bolts of lightning. They faded as he crept down, sweat running into his eyes.

He stood at last in the mouth of the passage, swaying on his feet. Timidly, Jarvey peeked out. The alley lay deserted, and he hurried back to the ramp and the cellar, wondering what fate he had just escaped. A scrawny arm reached out from the doorway, snagged his shirt, and dragged him inside before he could fight back or yell out.

It was one of the rangy kids—Jarvey dimly remembered that Betsy had called him Charley—who gave him a brown-toothed grin. "Nah, then, you don't wanna go out in the street. Not healthy, if you catch my meanin'."

Jarvey pulled away from the boy's grip. "What was going on? Those people?"

"Bein' driven to work, is all." Charley had an unruly mop of black hair. He brushed it out of his eyes and snuffled as if he had a cold, and carelessly wiped his nose with the back of his hand. "So you're a Midion, are you?"

"Yeah," Jarvey said unwillingly. "What about it?"

"Nothin', only"—Charley leaned close and lowered his voice, and his foul-smelling breath made Jarvey wince—"only, watch out for our Bets, if you know what's good for you. Full of plans, that one is, but she don't always think of what her plans might mean for the rest of us."

"O-okay," Jarvey muttered. "I—I'm going over here."

"Suit yourself," Charley said carelessly. "Me, I'm guardin' this here door for the time being. But you remember what I said, right? I don't know as how I'd trust Bets all that far. She's got a head on her, but she looks out for herself before she thinks of anybody else."

Jarvey clutched the book to his chest and stumbled away to the stack of crates that walled in the Den. Back inside, he crouched miserably in his corner.

Then, after what seemed like ages but really couldn't have been more than an hour, he heard a rattle of laughter. The blanket flipped aside, and six kids came running in, doubled over, each of them clutching something, all of them chuckling. One of them was Betsy. Charley sauntered through after her, smirking and smoothing his untidy black hair away from his forehead.

"Got your sleep in, then, did ya?" Betsy asked with a wide grin. "Time for eating, innit? Here, cully!"

She tossed something at him, something the size of a softball, and he caught it. It was round, or mostly round, with one flat side, and it was, as far as he could tell in the dimness, gray. "What is it?"

"Bread!" one of the boys snapped. "Lumme, Bets, this is a strange 'un and no mistake!"

Jarvey wrenched at the lump until it broke apart. It was bread of a sort, dense and heavy. He nibbled at it. Not much taste, but his empty stomach grumbled so loud that he wolfed it all down. "Here, wash it on its way," Betsy said, holding out a quart-sized bottle bound in brown leather strips. "Careful of that, now. Cost a lot o' slenkin', that did!"

It was tea, lukewarm and unsweetened, but that

didn't make any difference. Jarvey drank half the bottle, then when one of the other boys reached out, he handed it over. "Sl-slenkin'? What's that?" Jarvey asked.

"Whippin'! Nippin'! You know—stealin'!" Charley rolled his eyes. "You don't know nothing, do you?"

"Stealing?" Jarvey said, surprised. "You mean— didn't you—don't you have any money?"

"Left my brass in my other trousers, I did," the boy with the bottle, the one named Plum, said. "Green he is, Bets. Dump him, says I, or it's the Mill Press for you and him both, most like."

"What's the Mill Press?" Jarvey asked. "Look, I don't know who you are and I don't know where I am—"

"Leave us, you lot," Betsy said as a couple of the kids exchanged a dubious look. Then they all scrambled out, Charley herding the younger ones ahead of him. When they had gone, she sat beside

Jarvey. "All right, then, let's educate you. Have you been out and about enough to see anyone—anyone 'sides us, I mean?"

Jarvey's throat clenched. "This morning when I first woke up. I went outside."

"Not a good idea."

"I was going to see Lord Zoroaster, the man who talked to me about my parents. He lives somewhere called the Royal Crescent."

"Long way from here, Jarvey," Bets said. "And Lord Z ain't one of Nibs's favorites right now. Tryin' to see him, well, that might be dangerous."

"He told me he knew where my mom and dad are!" Jarvey said hotly. "I've got to find them. Anyway, I didn't go because there was a crowd of people in the streets. Some men in black leather coats were guarding them, and one of them—"

Betsy interrupted, "Yeah, shift change, that would've been. Right, then. Them's mill hands, see? When the tippers or the pressers find someone out past curfew, or when someone does somethin' out of line, or when the tippers just feel like it—"

"Tippers?"

"The men in black leather. Constables, police-men. The men all had clubs, right? Tipstaves, they call 'em. Tippers, see? Keeps order, they do. Any-way, the press goes by night, and the tippers by day, an' if they put hands on you, you go with them, see? Into the mills. And if you're as might be lucky, then you're there for maybe twenty years, if you can live that long, and then you get a second chance at obeying orders. Or if you're not lucky, you draw a life sentence, or more likely you die at the machines before your sentence is up, and then your troubles are over, right?"

"What mills?" Jarvey said. "What do they do?"

An angry, brooding expression crept into Betsy's face. For a moment she didn't answer, but took a drink from the bottle of tea. Then she growled, "In the mills they make things for the Toffs, mostly.

Clothes, furniture, fancy scents, jewelry. Some work in the cookeries, bakin' the bread, dressin' the meats, makin' the wines and all for the Toffs to eat. Sometimes we can slenk some, see? Nip into a storehouse or cookery, grab a bit o' bread or a pan of smoked fish, maybe. Get caught at that, it's life in the mills, but we don't get caught, 'cause we're Dodgers, see?"

"Who are the Toffs?" Jarvey asked.

"They owns Lunnon, don't they? They're in charge of the whole show, as you might say. Not more than a hundred of them, though, and the Lord Mayor, well you should know him right enough." She nudged him with an elbow. "They all call him Nibs, but not to his face, and his name's Tantalus Midion. You got his property there."

Jarvey felt as if his blood had chilled. "This, you mean?" he asked, holding up the Grimoire. "But I got this from an old man, Siyamon Midion, some kind of cousin or something. He took me to his house—"

"Aye, you said that last night. Look, cully, here's all I know about that. In the year of 1848, Tantalus Midion used the Grimoire to open up a pathway to this place. An' him an' his friends, the Toffs they are now, they brought people here an' made them work to build Lunnon as it is now."

"Then he must be dead."

"What makes you think that?"

"Because that was more than a hundred and fifty years ago!"

Betsy shook her head. "Don't work that way, cully. Look, there's time, see, an' there's book time. This here's book time, time created by the magic of that book there. The ones that come through from the other side of the book stay the same, see? They don't get no older. Their children, though, well, we grow up and grow old and we die, see? Don't ask me how it works. I don't have the art of it and couldn't tell you. Anyway, it's all account of the art and the book there."

"I don't know anything about that. Siyamon told me to look in the book, and it dragged me here somehow."

"That's the art working, see? The magic, I guess you'd call it. This Siyamon, he wanted to get rid of you for some reason, and he used the book to send you here. You were going to be a Transport. But here's the thing, see: Every Midion, so they say, writes his own chapter in that book. Every chapter leads to a different world, see? Your Midion, your Siyamon, must have been tryin' to send you to his chapter, not to ours. You tricked him, though. First one I ever heard of that got the best of a Midion, so good for you, cully."

"How did I trick him?" Jarvey asked.

"Well, see, you brought the book along with you. And that makes you valuable to Nibs and valuable to us, doesn't it? You know, some of the lot last night was for scragging you and—"

"What's that mean?"

"Killing you," she said with a shrug. "Scragging you and takin' the book. But no, I told 'em. I know the power of that thing. My own mother, see, she was Transported."

Jarvey shook his head and hoped his expression didn't look as dumb as he felt.

Irritation quirked the corner of Betsy's mouth. "Transported? Like you was. Brought here to Lunnon she was, from elsewhere, like all the first people. To help start old Midion's world, like. He used his book and he brought her here." Betsy balled her right hand into a fist and pounded it on her knee. "Mam hadn't done nothin' wrong, see? She just got caught by old Midion's lackeys, an' next thing she knows, she's through the book an' into Lunnon. Like all the firsts. My dad, well, I dunno. I think he was born here, though. He got Mill-Pressed when I was just a littl'un. You get Mill-Pressed, you don't get to talk to your family at all, and no news of you gets out, barrin' one of your mates gets released and dares to

83

tell your wife or husband about you. Nobody ever told Mam. Dad may be dead by now. Probably is."

Jarvey felt a faint stirring of hope. "Where's your mother?"

Betsy stood up. "Enough questions, cully."

Jarvey got to his feet, his face hot. "Look, don't keep calling me that, okay? I have a name. What's it mean, anyway? Cully?"

With a shake of her head, Betsy said, "Somebody green and not knowin'. Somebody a stranger, but not a threat. It's kind of matey, but kind of sneering, tell you truth. Not a bad name. But what do you want me to call you, then?"

"Jarvey will do."

"Right, then, Jarvey. Now look, do you know the spell of words to use to work that book or no? You said you didn't, but now it's just us, so tell me true."

"I don't know any magic," Jarvey said. "If I did, I wouldn't stay here another second."

"Know any of the art at all?"

Jarvey hesitated. Broken windows, blown light-bulbs, exploding baseball bats . . . melting candles. But he said gruffly, "I thought magic wasn't real. Just stuff in books and movies and like that. I never even believed in it until all this happened."

Betsy reached out and grabbed Jarvey's arm, hard. "Then you need help. All right. I need help, too. Trade's fair, innit?"

"Trade?"

Betsy leaned in close, her green eyes sharp enough to stab Jarvey to the soul. "My mother's in trouble. We'll do a deal. I'll take care of you, see, and make sure you don't get pressed, and teach you how to get food and drink, and help you find how to use that book. You're a Midion, you ought to be able to use the art, right? But when you do, see, you help me. You use your book to find my mother and set her free. Will you do that?"

"I-if I can."

Betsy gave a solemn nod. "Look, I believe in you. You have the blood of the Midions, and that's sorcery blood. They do say that some of 'em tried to use their art for good and not evil, but the bad 'uns, the ones like old Nibs—well, you stick with me, and we won't worry about him, right? We won't worry about them until you get strong enough to kill him."

Jarvey couldn't even swallow the lump that rose in his throat. He felt himself nod, and he felt his stomach clench, hard and heavy.

CHAPTER 5
The Free Folk

Royal Crescent was so far from the cellar that it took Bets, Charley, and Jarvey all morning to get there. They ducked along back alleys and streaked across busy streets, with Jarvey's head spinning. He tried to hide his fear as he followed in Bets's wake, slipping through streets clattering with horses, carts, and carriages.

"Here we are," Bets breathed at last. "Looks like there's some arrived ahead of us, though."

At the top of a low hill, they stood behind a hedge. Jarvey looked down a street paved with pale red brick and lined by waist-high, severely trimmed hedges. Down the hill, about a hundred yards away, two semicircular drives split off on either side of the street, and facing each drive was a magnificent curved three-story building with high, arched windows. Each building had three imposing doors. "Town houses for Toffs," Bets explained. "Six families there, all on the Council. Your Lord Zoroaster's is the closest one on the left, but see what's standing in front of it."

Three black carriages, each one drawn by two horses, had stopped at the curb. As Jarvey watched, the door to Number 3 opened and two men in black leather coats came out, arguing. At this distance, their voices were no more than an angry buzz, like a bee trapped in a glass jar.

"Come on," Bets said. "We'll get closer and see what's what. Charley, you stay here in case we need a decoy."

Jarvey followed her across the street, where they ducked behind the far hedge and crouched as they slipped down the hill. A rumble of wheels and the clopping of horses made them pause. Bets rose to take a quick look over the hedge, and Jarvey heard her suck in her breath. "It's him! Old Nibs! Come on!"

Bets wormed right into the base of the hedge, creeping easily among twisted gray branches in a kind of leaf-green twilight. Jarvey grunted as twigs caught his hair and clothing. Ahead of him, Bets stopped. Peering through the leaves, Jarvey spotted a coach, larger and far more magnificent than the others. The door bore a golden shield, and on the shield was the head of a wolf, in silver, with rubies for eyes.

One of the black-coated men appeared to open the door. Someone stirred in the dark interior of the coach, then stepped out into the strange milky light: a stooped, crooked old man, his face a sour, wrinkled apple framed by a fall of stringy white hair. Tantalus Midion, beyond any doubt. His dark blue eyes peered from beneath shaggy white brows, and his cheekbones lay knife-sharp beneath the skin.

Standing there leaning on an ebony cane, he looked enough like Siyamon to have been his brother.

"Well?" His voice was high, reedy, and cold.

The leather-jacketed man stood with his head bowed. "My lord, the man is not here."

"What do you mean?"

"He has gone away, my lord." The tipper's voice quivered.

With a snarl, Tantalus Midion raised his cane and struck the man a quick blow on the leg, making Jarvey wince. "You will find the traitor Zoroaster, or I shall have you put to death. I shall have you flayed alive, boiled in oil, torn to pieces, and fed to the ravens. Do you understand me?" He had not raised his voice from a conversational level.

"Yes, my lord."

The old man growled, swiveling his head, sniffing the air. "Something odd is happening. Something here is not in order. Zoroaster left my Council without permission, and the palace guards say he took a servant with him. He brought no servant into my house, and Zoroaster is a secret man. He shares his carriage with no one."

The tipper was sweating. "No, my lord."

Tantalus Midion raised his bony hand, his fingers slipping against his thumb, as though he were feeling the atmosphere. "The air feels wrong here. Something is disturbing the fabric of my city. Zoroaster would be able to tell me what the problem is. Scour the entire city, man. Find Zoroaster and bring him to me. I will crush his secrets from him."

"Yes, my lord."

"The air is wrong," Tantalus repeated. "If Zoroaster dares to challenge me—let it be known to all that I can destroy this city if I must. I have days of life left to me on Earth. I could return there, retrieve the Book, and make another world if I chose. If I did that, I would rip out this chapter, and you and everyone else would perish. Do you understand? Be advised. Find the man." With that, the old man turned and stepped back into the carriage. The tipper closed the door, and the driver whipped the horses into motion.

As soon as the carriage had driven away, the tipper groaned, limped to the edge of the drive, and vomited in the gutter. Jarvey shivered.

Other tippers appeared from the doorway of Number 3, each one forcing a man or woman ahead of him. "We haven't seen the master since yesterday," one old man protested.

The tipper steering him slapped him hard. "Quiet until we ask! Sir, this is the lot."

The tipper who had spoken to Tantalus wiped his mouth. "Take the servants to the lockup to be questioned."

Jarvey counted six of them in all, two men, one old woman, and three middle-aged women, all of them weeping. The tippers forced them into the carriages, and then the carriages rolled away.

"Let's go," Bets said.

Their trip back to the cellar was somber. Bets muttered, "If Nibs is after Lord Z, you'd best keep your distance from the man. Lord Z might be strong, but Nibs would snap him like a matchstick. Looks like you got no one to help you find your parents but us, Jarvey."

Charley slapped him on the shoulder. "Don't worry. We'll find your mam and dad for you. If we have to, we'll leave the city until this hunt for Lord Z ends one way or the other. We've stayed in the Wild before this."

"Won't come to that if I can help it," Bets returned. "It's no life in the Wild."

"What's the Wild?" Jarvey asked, not sure if he really wanted to know.

Bets shrugged. "Well, there's Lunnon, and there's the farmlands all about, see? And the rest of the whole world, that's the Wild. Strange trees that talk at night, animals that might've been humans until Nibs got mad at 'em, mountains that move, ground that sucks you down under and smothers you. It's poison land, land that's almost alive. Most of the farmers, they're people who are glad enough to be out of the tippers' sight and striking, but every year a few of them are taken off by the things that live in the Wild. Besides, if you run into the Wild to get away from Nibs, and he finds out about it, he comes after you."

"Hunts runaways for sport, Nibs does," Charley said with a brown-toothed grin. "In the palace— that's Bywater House, where he lives—they do say he has a room with their heads hangin' up on the walls."

"Just talk, but we'll try to keep well out of the Wild," Bets said. "Charley, spread the word. Tomorrow noon we have a meeting with the other bands."

"Why?" Charley asked, sounding surprised.

"Nibs thinks something's here as shouldn't be here. That's Jarvey, innit? Sooner we help him find his parents and get out of Lunnon, sooner the tippers will ease off."

Charley just grunted. Jarvey tried to say "Thanks," but the word wouldn't come out. He wasn't sure that Bets could really help him. Or that she planned to.

Another sleepless, fearful night, another morning under a pale, milky sky, and Jarvey began to despair of ever seeing his mother or father again. After a hasty breakfast, he took the Grimoire off into a corner and tried to open it.

The latch refused to give. Maybe you had to have that circle around it, he thought. Or give the book a command. "Open," he said.

Nothing happened.

"I command you to open!" he growled, feeling foolish.

He reached for the latch, and with a crackle an angry red spark burned his fingers. He jerked his hand away, yelping. His thumb and two of his fingers showed white blisters the size of pencil erasers. Jarvey felt a flare of frustration and anger inside.

He grabbed the book and made a hasty retreat to the Den.

By noon, thirty or more ragged, dirty kids had gathered in the basement. Most of them clustered in a loose group, with only Charley apart, standing beside the door with his arms crossed and a resigned smile on his thin face. Betsy stood on one of the rusted machines and had them all take a good look at Jarvey. "He's a new one, but he's game to join the Free Folk," she announced. "Spread the word. He's Jarvey Green to everyone, right? And he's to have help from any of the Free Folk, on my say."

"Got a mum or dad lookin' for him, has he?" asked an older boy, dressed in a shabby old coat and a battered felt hat.

"He's lost his parents," Betsy said shortly.

"Lumme," little Puddler squeaked. "Becomin' a orphan without permission? That's an automatic life sentence in the mills, that is!"

"Half of us are guilty of it, though, so what's the

difference?" a plain-faced, red-haired girl said, to a general murmur of agreement.

"All right," Betsy said. "That's one thing I want you all to do: Keep your ears and eyes open for strange new folk in Lunnon, a man and a woman, Jarvey's parents. If they're here, someone will notice them. They'll stand out. You'll know if you get word of them, and if you do, you come to me, understand?"

There was a general murmur of agreement, and then Bets continued, "Now, Jarvey's not used to life outside, so he's got to lay low until he gets the hang of things. So me and some of my Dodgers are goin' on the sly with him to give him a bit of training. Can't stay here, because it's too close to the tippers' den over in Dead Street, so we'll be moving on."

"Where will you den, then?" someone asked.

Betsy hardly spared him a glance. "New place. Never you mind where it is. We don't want any of you lot gettin' nipped and bargaining for your free-dom with our secrets, right?"

"Oi!" shouted the oldest boy. "None of that, Bets. We're Free Folk, we are. Death before dis-honor." Jarvey saw the black-haired Charley, in the background, shake his head as if in disbelief.

"Bets?" another kid, a fourteen- or a fifteen-year-old boy, asked in a hesitant, hopeful tone. "If you and the Dodgers are thinkin' about movin' out of this place, how's it if my lot take up here? The tippers are sniffing awfully close to our digs in the attic of the sick-house down by the river. Besides that, it ain't healthy, over there where so many go to die."

"Take it, then, and welcome," Betsy said. "Only don't come in from the wide street by day, not ever. The alley's the only way then. Tell you what, we'll leave Charley for a few days to show you the ins and outs, how's that?"

"Bag that up and sell it!" Charley snapped. "You ain't ditchin' me, Bets."

"No," Betsy agreed. "You'll come along to you-know-where in a couple of days, after Ben's bunch settle in here. You're the best one to teach them, and you know it. So you stay, and that's that."

Charley leaned back against the brick wall, arms still crossed, head lowered and a scowl on his face. Uneasily, Jarvey wondered if Betsy somehow knew about the warning Charley had given him. Was she trying to separate Charley from the group because he knew things that she didn't want Jarvey to learn?

Betsy fielded more questions, and Jarvey listened with his head spinning. In all his life he'd never been involved in anything more serious than a hard-fought game of baseball, but these kids played for their lives, every day and every night. He nervously fingered the book wrapped up in his old shirt. He wore clothes like the other kids now, given to him by Betsy. The buttonless pullover shirt, coarse as burlap and a dreary gray, hung on him like a tent. He wore faded black pants, their legs loose and floppy, hacked off short three inches above his ankles. The only things of his own that he kept were his sneakers. He felt ridiculous in that getup, but mostly nervous about all those eyes staring at his face, filing away images of him for future reference.

As Betsy dealt with the group's curiosity, Jarvey gratefully sank down and sat, glad to be out of the spotlight. He wondered what had become of Zoroaster and what Zoroaster knew about the Grimoire. The weight of the book seemed to be increasing, and just touching its covers gave Jarvey a peculiarly cold, sick feeling. He hated the thing and wished he could throw it away, but it seemed to be his only hope.

Jarvey tried to make sense of the fragments Zoroaster had told him. When Siyamon Midion had used his dark art on Mom and Dad, what had happened to them? Were they enslaved in one of the deadly mills?

Maybe the clues he needed were inside the

book—but if the book wouldn't allow itself to be read . . .

But he was a Midion, and even old Siyamon had said he had the art. How could he use it, though? How did the evil Midion sorcerers learn the magic they had? He didn't know and couldn't even guess.

Jarvey forced himself to listen to the debate in the cellar. Betsy was again urging caution to the boy who'd asked for use of the Den.

"Stop your worryin'. We ain't never been nipped yet," the boy Betsy had called Ben said with an air of confidence. "No fear of that. And any time you want to come back, we'll find another snug. Thanks, Bets."

Betsy nodded, though she still looked doubt-ful. "Well, then. We'll move out come good dark tonight. That's it, then, but I want you all to take one last look at the new boy. Jarvey, up here."

Hands helped boost him, and Jarvey scrambled up onto the machine to stand beside Betsy. He tugged at the gray shirt, far too big for him, and felt acutely aware of sixty or more eyes staring at him.

"Last time, now, so get a good look," Betsy said. "Look at the face, not the togs. Be ready to tell the rest of the folk what he looks like, and send along word to them he's protected, right? Another thing, if anybody hears of anybody calling themselves Americans in Lunnon, you get word to me, quick. Same if anybody gets word of Lord Zoroaster. This could be our chance at last."

"Chance to do what?" one older boy demanded.

Betsy's green eyes flashed. "Chance to get rid of the Toffs and the tippers. Chance to be free. Chance to pull down old Nibs from his seat on the bent backs of our people."

"Chance to be free," a solemn-looking girl of fourteen or fifteen said.

"Chance to be free," Betsy agreed.

Jarvey saw the kids in the room nod to each other, heard them murmur. It wasn't a cheer, it wasn't a surge of enthusiasm, but it felt deep and powerful.

And Betsy seemed satisfied. "All right," she said in a hard, level voice. "You know what we risk. You know what we have to gain. Scatter, now, and spread the word."

Like a magic trick—or like the workings of a spell of art, Jarvey supposed—the thirty kids flowed away, rustling out of the basement, fading into the shadows.

Betsy gave Jarvey a crooked grin. "And you," she said, "I hope you're a quick learner."

CHAPTER 6
Life on the Run

At first Jarvey tried to keep count of the days that followed, but somewhere around three weeks, he stopped tracking them. One day was just like the day before, with the only changes being the number of close calls. Every single day brought too many of them.

The new Den was in yet another narrow brick-walled alley. Both entrances to this one had been bricked up ages ago, so now it was a long, cramped room, roofed over because the eaves of the buildings on either side met overhead. From the street you'd never guess the space existed, because the brickwork that sealed it had the same crumbling, sooty appearance of the buildings to either side. Getting in and out took some trouble. You had to duck down into a storm drain—there were two of these, front door and back door, as Betsy called them—and then creep along hunched over for a hundred feet or so until you could pop up through an open drain in the center of the alley. Once a heavy barred iron grate had covered it, but the Free Folk had moved that aside.

"Biggest danger's that someone'll notice us slipping into the drain and follow us in one day," Betsy told everyone. "So we can't treat this like the old Den. Two have to stay inside at all times, and if a stranger pops his head up, they take care of him."

Jarvey had not asked what "taking care of him" might mean. He didn't even want to know. He began to have a strange feeling as days passed: that his old life, his real life, was just a half-forgotten dream, and that he had awakened from it into this nightmare world of no electricity, no comforts, and no family. The walled-off alley proved a bleak shelter, cold and dark, and incredibly, Jarvey thought back to the basement of the abandoned factory with a kind of regret. It had running water and light, anyway.

The other kids were patient enough with him, and even cheerful in their strange way. Charley Dobbins, when he returned from the first Den, turned out to be a good teacher, and he personally took charge of Jarvey's street education. They ventured out every day, and every day Jarvey saw more signs that this was not his own world. Even on clear days, no sun shone in the sky—there was just a sort of blurred brassy circle of light and warmth, many times larger than the sun he remembered. No moon pierced the gloom at night, and even the stars were strange.

Under the metallic glare of daylight, the two of them sauntered through alleys and down back ways, armed with little squares of pasteboard that Betsy provided. These were work cards, which told the world that Jarvey and Charley were kitchen boys on the evening shift in one of the cookeries. "These'll do for anybody but a tipper," Charley had warned, raising his hand to swipe the hair out of his eyes. "Never show a tipper your ticket, or you'll get nipped sure's anything. But if anybody else gives you any bother, just flash it and tell 'em you're off work right now and runnin' some errands for Master Cook, right?"

As long as they didn't go out after curfew, the two boys could wander around the crowded streets with something like invisibility. The beaten-down people creeping to or from work seemed too exhausted even to give them a glance, and the Toffs pointedly ignored them. Jarvey soon got the hang of recognizing the Toffs, the well-dressed men and women whose carriages rumbled over the cobblestones, drawn by horses that looked healthier than most of the people. Now and again, Charley would grandly rush to open a door for a rich-looking man and woman, sweeping his cap away from his tangled hair and crooning, "Remember the porter, governor!" And sometimes, not very often, the man would drop a small coin into his cap without looking directly at the dirty, grinning Charley. With a wink, Charley said, "Never go for a man alone, or worse a woman alone, mate. Couples are the ticket. A man wants to show off a bit before his lady, see? A woman alone, she'd scream for a tipper, and a gent alone would clout you with his walkin' stick. But couples, they're easy pickings."

The two boys could wander into a storehouse where wagons of vegetables or pastries waited to be unloaded, with Charley bawling, "Robertson? Got a message for a Robertson! Robertson, are you here?"

And sometimes a Robertson would call out, "Hey, over here!" It always turned out to be the wrong one, though. Charley would ask, "Are you Artemus Fairweather Robertson, then?" No, he was Bob Robertson, or George Robertson, or some other Robertson. While Charley created the diversion, Jarvey would snatch something, a couple of apples, even a head of cabbage, while no one was looking. A cabbage was dinner. Potatoes were a celebration. A sweet roll was heaven.

Nights chilled them in the walled-off alley, because their fire had to be very small. Gradually the kids of Betsy's gang accumulated blankets, old cast-off rags, even bolts of cloth stolen from under the Toffs' noses, to create a kind of unruly nest where they could all burrow for warmth.

But Betsy was a hard, demanding leader. At night, when Jarvey felt ready to drop, she would have him tell her about his day, criticize his decisions and his movements, and demand that he think of some way to use the book.

"I can't," he told her one evening weeks after they had made their move. "Look." He pulled the book from its hiding place and handed it to her. "Open it," he told her.

She jerked her hands off the book as if it had suddenly caught fire. "You crazy, Jarvey? This thing could send me to—"

"Try," Jarvey said wearily. "You'll see what I mean."

Betsy was nothing if not brave. She glared at him, the firelight gleaming in her green eyes, and then said, "Right, then." She took one deep breath, grasped the book, and then drew in a sharp gasp of surprise. "What's wrong with it?"

"You can't open it," Jarvey told her. "I can't either."

"It's like a solid block," Betsy said, running her finger over the edges of the book's pages. "Like it's glued shut. Reckon it takes art to open?"

"It must take something," Jarvey said. "But I don't know what it is. And I can't think of any way of finding out, except one." He shivered. He didn't want Betsy to ask the question that he knew she would ask.

"What's that?"

"It's the Midion Grimoire," he said in a low, unwilling voice. "And you said one person here knows how to use it."

"Nibs," Betsy said with a worried nod. "But he's a terror, he is. You can't walk up and ask old Nibs how to use the thing."

"There's Lord Zoroaster."

Betsy shook her head. "He's melted into air, it seems. Nibs ain't found him, and none o' the Free Folk have heard a whisper about him. Nor of any Americans. Sorry, Jarvey. I could've sworn we'd turn up Lord Z or your parents by this time."

"Then there's only Bywater House," Jarvey said.

Betsy leaned forward, hugging her knees. "Tall order, Jarvey. Things here, well, I don't think they're like they were back where you come from. You keep talking about things that seem like art to me, tell-a-visions and movie and whatnot. Well, old Midion does use the art of magic. He's likely to have guard spells up around his mansion to keep out the likes of you and me, and if not that, he's got ranks of guards."

"I'll have to take the risk," Jarvey said. "Look, I was in Bywater House once, and I got out without Tantalus turning me into a frog."

Betsy frowned and shook her head. "Nobody in their right mind would try what you're suggesting. It could be like walkin' into a death trap." In a thoughtful tone, she added, " 'Course, he ain't always in the house. When the Council's not meeting, sometimes Nibs goes up the river to his country house. He likes . . . hunting."

"Maybe we could have a chance if we could get into Bywater House while he's away," Jarvey said slowly.

"I'll think on it some," Betsy said. She handed the heavy book back to Jarvey. "Meantime, you keep this safe."

"I will."

For some days everything rested there. But then it happened.

The blow fell early one morning, down by the wharves. Betsy, Charley, Jarvey, and half a dozen others of the gang idled by the docks where boats delivered cattle and sheep from somewhere upriver. Everything stank of manure and sweat, but Jarvey had learned to ignore the stench. Like the others, he concentrated on their target, a round-bowed green boat loaded down with huge barrels overflowing with speckled yellow pears and shining red apples.

Charley was in charge of the raiding party, and at a nod from him, Puddler and Plum and two others jumped with him onto the boat. Instantly one of the men on the dock, a big thick-necked fellow, roared a curse and raised a threatening fist.

"Get off there! Get off there!" Betsy bellowed, running up after Charley. "Oh, sir, my brother's not right in the head, please don't hit him!" She clung to the man's arm, and real tears ran down her face.

"Get off my boat!" the man yelled, shaking his free fist. "Here, let go of me!"

"Somebody help!" Betsy shouted, dangling from the big man's arm like a doll. "You lot, get him! Don't hurt him, he's not in his right mind!"

Jarvey and two other of the boys jumped to the deck, and Puddler joined them in tugging at Charley. "Come on, come on," Puddler urged with a wink at Jarvey. "We know you love pears, but these ain't yours to eat."

The boys' shirts, belted at the waist, already bulged suspiciously with fruit, but Charley grabbed two pears and stuck one more into his gaping mouth. "Gd!" he said in a fruit-muffled voice. "'S gd!"

"Drop them!" the man yelled as the others pretended to hustle Charley back onto the dock. Jarvey saw that the boat owner wasn't going to get any help from the other boatmen, who were pointing and laughing and clearly enjoying the show.

Betsy pleaded, "Sir, let him keep them! I—I'll run home and fetch you the money. Pray, sir, my mother is very ill, and poor Adelbert isn't in his right mind, and—"

The man finally shook her off and glared after the retreating group of boys, already at the mouth of an alley. "Oh, get along with you," he thundered. "But if any of you gang show your noses around here again, I'll break 'em for you, understand?"

Murmuring thanks, Betsy ran after the boys— and as soon as she joined them in the alley, she broke into laughter. "Charley, you should be on a stage, and no mistake," she chortled. "You can act a fool better than anybody I know."

Jarvey laughed for the first time in what felt like weeks.

"Stop your mouth with that," Charley crowed back, tossing Betsy a yellow pear. "Got enough for a right feast here, haven't we, boys?"

"Half a bushel!" Puddler shot back, hefting the

apples and pears he had stuffed down inside his baggy shirt.

And then they emerged from the alley and saw the tippers, four of them, brandishing their staves and grinning. "Got 'em," one of the big men said softly, tapping his staff in his left hand. "Round 'em up and we'll have 'em before the magistrate."

Betsy hit Jarvey hard on the back. "Scatter!"

Apples and pears rolled underfoot. The gang flew headlong down the alley, with the tippers in hot pursuit. Their hobnailed boots rang on the cobbles, and Jarvey ran harder than he had ever run before.

They burst out onto the wharves, Puddler diving to the right, Betsy and Charley to the left. Jarvey felt a hand swipe down his back, just missing him. Without thinking, he made a jump for the deck of the fruit ship. The owner howled in rage.

Whirling, Jarvey grabbed a couple of apples. The tipper behind him was tangled with the boatman. Jarvey's heart sank as he saw one of the black-clad tippers grab Betsy and lift her, kicking and shrieking, into the air. The tipper shoved the boatman away and started to take the long step onto the boat deck.

Jarvey wound up and pitched, a fast apple to the face. The fruit smacked into the tipper's scarlet forehead, and with a bellow, he missed his step, tumbling from the dock into the water. Jarvey kicked back and threw the second apple at the tipper carrying Betsy, but he was too far away and the missile fell short. Another tipper was blowing furiously on a whistle, and from down the wharves more of them showed up, coming at a steady trot. One of them pointed toward Jarvey.

There was no way to escape—tippers closed in from left and right.

Maybe there was *one* way: Jarvey leaped to the far side of the boat. The river was wide here, fifty yards across, and it looked deep. Jarvey threw himself off the deck, lowered his head, and felt the cold shock of water as he dived in.

He plunged deep below the surface, holding his breath desperately. Using a kind of breaststroke, Jarvey followed the current, vaguely aware of the looming shadows of boats off to his right and over-head. Bars of green-tinged daylight streaked through the water.

His lungs burned, but Jarvey forced himself to stay under. Another stroke, another, and another. He had gone incredibly far, farther than he should have been able to swim underwater, but he had to breathe.

Instead, he blew bubbles and made himself swim under a boat, into the dark water under the pilings of a dock. At last he let himself come up, and the moment his head broke the surface, he gulped in a lungful of blessed air.

Then he dived again and made his way still far-ther downstream. When he dared to come up a second time, he couldn't hear any commotion. For a moment, Jarvey clung to the rough wood of a piling.

Then, with infinite caution, he pulled himself up so he could peer over the edge of the wharf.

This dock lay empty, and so was the next one, but then the boats began. Far down the line, he saw a crowd of tippers. One was stomping around and streaming water—the one who had fallen in the river, Jarvey decided. The others bent over, holding on to their captives. He couldn't tell how many of the gang they had caught. Two other tippers stood on the deck of the fruit boat and leaned far over as they repeatedly plunged long hooked poles down in the water.

Fishing for me, he thought. They think I drowned back there.

He began to shiver. For five or ten minutes he watched, and then the black-clad tippers turned away. A mob of them dragged at least two or three of the gang into the alley. Three or four others stood around talking to the boatmen.

They weren't looking his way. Jarvey slipped

across the wharves. The buildings here were all warehouses. The handiest one sported a rusty old ladder leading up the wall to its flat roof. Jarvey didn't even hesitate. He closed his hands on the rough rungs and pulled himself up. He felt a desperate strength in his arms, and something, some power, seemed to creep over his skin like a million busy ants. Steam curled from his sodden clothing. By the time he reached the roof, his clothes felt bone-dry. Wild art, he supposed. It couldn't be the Grimoire, hidden back in the Den, but simple magic like this wouldn't help him save the gang.

The warehouses had been built so close together that getting from one roof to the next was at most a short jump, and usually just a long step. Crouching, hurrying, Jarvey set off in the direction of the alley. He couldn't let the tippers take away his only friends.

At least not without a fight.

CHAPTER 7
Hot Pursuit

On the flat roof of another warehouse, Jarvey lay on his stomach and peered down at the cobblestoned street. Brassy yellow daylight lay over everything, casting weak, fuzzy shadows. Below, on the far side of the street, a few well-dressed Toffs ate at outdoor tables, laughing and chatting. No traffic moved in the street—none except a boxy green carriage, drawn by two midnight-black horses. As it slowly rumbled past, Jarvey could see the rear of the carriage, enclosed in iron bars, like a cage, and three pairs of hands gripping the bars. Shadows hid everything else inside the cage.

A driver wearing the black leather uniform of a tipper hunched like a disgruntled vulture in the driver's seat, one beefy red hand clutching the reins, the other a whip. Behind him, on a seat up on the roof of the carriage, two more black-clad tippers sat, their heads swiveling constantly as they scanned the alleys and street. Once the wagon had rolled past, Jarvey stood up and looked uncertainly ahead. He had two more flat roofs, and then he faced a wide space that he couldn't hope to jump across.

Scrambling to the edge of the roof, Jarvey judged the distance to the next one, backed away again, and took a long broad jump across to the roof on the far side of the alley. He hit hard on his heels and tumbled forward, catching himself on outthrust hands, and pushed himself back up. At the far side of the roof he looked down: a two-story drop, too far to leap. But a black iron drainpipe ran down the wall at the rear of the building.

Jarvey swung himself over the edge of the roof and locked his legs around the drain where it slanted away from the roof and down toward the wall. With an effort, Jarvey got his hands on it and eased down. Climbing was hard, hanging at a backward forty-five-degree angle like a sloth, but then it got harder. The drain pipe had been fastened to the bricks with iron straps, and Jarvey couldn't keep a grip all the way around it. He half slid and half fell twenty feet, landing on a squelchy, stinking mess around the foot of the drain, a mound of dirt, leaves, and garbage.

He edged forward in the dark alley, wondering if the tippers' wagon had caught up to him. No, he could hear the slow clop-clop of the horses from away to his left. The three tippers were probably still looking for other members of the gang. The wagon wouldn't race. They had all the time in the world.

Jarvey sank back into the shadows and watched the horses and wagon lumber past in a long streak of black and green, and then he chanced a look outside. His heart sank as he saw Betsy's face up against the bars, and next to her little Puddler's. He couldn't make out who the third captive was.

When the wagon turned right far down at the corner, Jarvey darted out of the alley and sprinted. If a Toff noticed him, he'd yell that he was an errand boy and couldn't stop. If a tipper saw him, well, he'd worry about that when it happened.

Around the corner, and he spotted the wagon standing still a block ahead. The driver had pulled over to the curb on a street of small stone homes with sharp-pitched roofs. Jarvey slunk along until he came to a rain barrel standing against the brick wall of the last warehouse. He hid behind the barrel and took everything in. The cobbled street sloped downhill to the edge of the river, but here the stream stretched shore to shore with no wharves or docks. A few small white triangular sails, sails of pleasure boats, glided far upstream, too distant to be a source of worry or help.

"The others had to've come this way," Jarvey

heard one of the tippers grumble in a harsh voice. He peeked around the barrel and saw all three of the tippers, the driver and two guards, standing on the sidewalk next to the horses. "Four or five of 'em at least."

"We looked in every alley and didn't see no sign of 'em," another one said. "They've scattered by now. Took too much time haulin' old Saunders out of the river, the fool. I say we take these three in and forget about the others. We got ways of catchin' rats, and we'll nip 'em sooner or later, anyhow."

"No." The third voice was the hard, stern voice of authority. Jarvey blinked. It belonged to a man who wore exactly the same uniform as the others. He wore no badge of office or mark of distinction, but the man's face was cold, with a hawk's bill of a nose, eyes that glared from deep caverns under straight, heavy black brows, and a long, sharp chin. Jarvey settled back on his heels as the tipper turned his head slowly, scanning the street. As he did, Jarvey saw a jagged scar across his right cheek. The man was blind in his right eye.

For a moment the tipper's baleful one-eyed gaze paused, and Jarvey tensed to run for his life, sure that he'd been spotted. But then the man's head snapped around to his two comrades. "No," he said again. "They must still be here somewhere, hiding. We'll walk down the wharves. We'll check every warehouse and every alley again from this side. Saunders and the others are on River Street by this time. They will make sure these rats don't slip away from us and get out that way."

"You sure about that, Cap'n?" one of the others asked sarcastically. "Old Saunders took quite a duckin' in the river, didn't he? He was squallin' about gettin' to the lockup and changing clothes."

"If he's not guarding the alleys, he'll find himself in front of a loom tomorrow," the leader said. "Come, you two. Tie up the horses and come."

He and one of the other tippers vanished, walking past the far end of the warehouse on the narrow drive on the riverside. The third, still grumbling, tied the horses to a lamppost, then followed.

As soon as he was gone, Jarvey dashed to the wagon. "Betsy!" he whispered.

"Jarvey?" Betsy's face split into a grin. "Welcome sight you are! Quick, get us out of this."

Jarvey looked helplessly at the ponderous iron lock. "I don't have the key!"

Billis, a quiet boy about Betsy's age, said hoarsely, "Look up front, Jarv. See if the driver's seat raises up. Usually there's a compartment underneath 'em, and sometimes they chucks the keys in there."

Jarvey tiptoed around the far side of the wagon and climbed up into the driver's position. The two horses heard him, and both stamped their feet and whinnied. Jarvey tugged at the seat, swung it up, and found only a heavy wool coat in the compartment underneath it. He swung the seat back into place and started to jump down when—

"Oi! Off from there!" It was one of the tippers, two hundred feet away, pointing and shouting.

Jarvey had a split second to make a decision. He jumped down, untied the reins—they had just been loosely looped around the lamppost—and then scrambled back up in the driver's seat, snatching the whip from its socket. "Come on!" Jarvey yelled. He didn't know how to use the whip, but he flicked its length, and the tip of the wooden staff grazed the rear end of the horse on the left. The black horse flinched in surprise and then started to clop, and the other joined it, jerking the wagon ahead in a clattering roll toward the river.

"Stop! Hey, you two, help me!" The tipper belatedly broke into a waddling run, waving his arms and bellowing.

Jarvey hauled on the reins, and the horses obediently pulled the wagon in a wide U-turn, heading back up the hill. The fat tipper was getting close to them—

"Get up!" Jarvey shouted, snapping the reins.

The horses seemed to understand. Both of them broke into a fast walk, and with another flick of the reins, into something like a gallop. The wagon clunked and bumped over the cobblestones, jolting and lurching, and Jarvey fell backward in the seat. He struggled back up again. They were up the hill, leaving the shouting, red-faced tipper shaking his fist at the corner down near the river.

The street leveled out, but still the horses did not slow. The wagon flashed past a garden party of Toffs playing croquet on a green lawn behind a black wrought-iron fence. The players straightened and stared at the wagon with round, startled eyes. Jarvey grimaced. How did you steer horses? The team was in a hurry to get somewhere, but he couldn't control them. Jarvey hauled again on the reins with desperate strength until the horses got the message. They slowed, but then took an unexpected sharp left turn into a narrower street.

Jarvey felt the wagon tilt up onto two wheels, and as it toppled he vaulted free, landing hard on his shoulder and rolling. With a splintering crash, the wagon smashed into the corner of a brick shop. Jarvey pushed himself up to see the horses tear themselves free of the wreck and go cantering away, still yoked together, their iron-shod hoofs striking sparks from the cobblestones. He scuttled to the rear of the wagon. "Are you okay?"

Inside the cage the three captives struggled in a mass of arms and legs. Then Betsy got herself free. "Help me here! Come on, Jarvey, quick!"

Betsy was struggling with the door. Jarvey reached for the lock and shook it in frustration.

A young woman in a bonnet and a long gray dress had come out of the shop and stood with her hand clasped to her chest. "You frightened the life out of us! What is the meaning of this?" she snapped, her face red.

"Ow!" Betsy had jerked her hands away from the

bars and shook them as if she had touch
stove.

In Jarvey's hands the lock crawled with crackling silver sparks. He couldn't let go of it. He clenched his teeth.

Betsy, Puddler, and Billis shoved the door open, knocking Jarvey onto his seat as they struggled out. Betsy grabbed his hand and hauled him to his feet. "Run! Split and run to the Den. If I'm not there by dark, scatter and it's everyone for himself. Tell the others, and run!"

Already a loose group of men was jogging toward them—not tippers, but well-dressed men running from the shops and the markets. Jarvey fled from them, reached a row of humble-looking houses, and dived behind them, jumping fences and ducking through backyard gardens until he was out of the residential area.

The factories began, and Jarvey felt a rush of relief. Charley had taught him how to hide in streets like these. He rushed into the first alley he reached, not even thinking that once he had been afraid of such narrow, dark places.

"There's one of 'em!"

The alley lay straight between two streets. Two tippers stood at the far end, and they pounded toward him. Jarvey backpedaled.

He was younger, but he was winded. They gained on him. He reached the end of the alley—

A hand closed on his arm and jerked him to one side. Jarvey fought back, pummeling the man who had seized him—

"Stand absolutely still and do not make a sound!"

Jarvey gasped. Zoroaster! The man chanted something under his breath, something that Jarvey could not make out.

The world plunged into darkness.

"Still and quiet, for your life!" Zoroaster whispered.

Jarvey obeyed.

CHAPTER 8
The Rat

Jarvey felt as if he were suffocating. Everything had gone absolutely dark, darker than midnight. He felt Zoroaster's hand shove him back against the brick building, and he stood gasping for air.

A moment later, boots clapped on the cobblestones. "Which way did he go?" a hoarse voice demanded.

"Can't see 'im now," the other tipper returned. "Must've cut across there and into Crooked Alley."

"You sure?"

"No place on the street for 'im to hide, is there? Come on!"

Running footsteps faded in the distance, died

away. The hand on Jarvey's arm dragged him sideways, and he stumbled, unable to see where they were going. Then he heard Zoroaster chant again, and in a blinding flood the brassy daylight returned.

Zoroaster stood beside him, his left hand grasping Jarvey's right arm, his right hand flat on the alley wall. The man had changed. His hair had been cropped short, and he wore ragged gray clothing, like a commoner. "It's lucky I've been watching for you," he said. "Are you all right?"

"Wh-what did you do?" Jarvey asked.

"I made us both invisible," Zoroaster snapped. "We'll have to move. Midion can detect magic. You did a bit a few minutes ago, and I just did considerably more."

"Invisible?" Jarvey gasped. "I couldn't see!"

"Of course not. If you are invisible, the retinas of your eyes are transparent. If that is so, no image can form upon them. That is a disadvantage of invisibility. Follow me."

They trotted down the alley, into another street, and then beneath a short arched bridge, where they paused. Jarvey hadn't realized how out of breath the pursuit had made him. His legs felt as if the bones had become jelly. "What—what happened after that night?" he asked. "Why did you run away?"

"I ran because Tantalus knew you had left with me, and because I had seen the Grimoire," Zoroaster said. "He does not know it is here. He must not know. If he were close to capturing me, I would choose death rather than giving him the knowledge of the book's whereabouts." Zoroaster passed a hand across his face, as if he were terribly tired. "What did you do? I felt something of it, the energy, but not what kind of spell you performed."

"I—I unlocked a lock," Jarvey said. "My friends had been caught, and I made the lock unfasten itself."

"How?"

"I don't know," Jarvey confessed. "I was holding

it, and I kept telling it to unlock. Not out loud, I just thought it. And sparks shot from it, and then it just opened."

"Extraordinary," Zoroaster said. "Most beginners cannot focus without the discipline of a spoken spell."

"Then once before—" Jarvey hesitated, then told of how he had climbed up the narrow alley and how the tipper had looked straight at him without appearing to see him. "I thought I was invisible then," he finished.

"No," Zoroaster said. "You were simply not noticed—that is not the same thing as being truly invisible. You may have caused the tipper to become inattentive, to ignore you. That is easy to do with one person, but almost impossible with two or more."

"Listen," Jarvey said, "you were going to find my mom and dad. Have you—"

"No." The word was harsh and final. "No, Jarvey,

I have not found them. Believe me, I have inquired every way I know how, and that includes some ways even Tantalus could not guess. Only one person can find them now."

"Who?"

"You," Zoroaster said. "I will have to ask you not to try, though. Not yet, anyway."

"What?"

"Because you will have to use the Grimoire." Zoroaster had lowered his voice to a harsh whisper. "And I do not know what opening that cursed volume would do, here, in the very land it shaped for Tantalus Midion. I have been in its presence five times, six counting the time I saw it in your hands. I lack the courage of some sorcerers, however. I have never had the courage to open the book. For in opening it, in reading the dire spells it contains, one's will may be warped, one's soul turned toward evil. The promise of power is a terrible temptation."

"I can't open it," Jarvey said. "I've tried."

"Don't try again! Not unless I tell you to do so."

Jarvey stepped away from him, balling his fists at his sides. "If I can find my mom and dad by opening the book, I'll open it!"

"I'm not sure you can," Zoroaster said. "Yet there seems to be no other way. Listen: Tantalus's men have come close to me, far too close for my peace of mind. I may have to leave Lunnon, to go outside."

"Outside?"

"Into the real world. Yes, I can move back and forth, though it is very dangerous. If I must, then Tantalus will know I have left, and he may work spells to block me from returning. Yet I know of no other way to find the essential spells that might allow you to open the Grimoire and survive. Do you know Green Park, at the corner of Broad and Brick streets?"

"I could find it."

"At the center of the park is a fountain. If I can learn what I need to know, I will meet you there."

"How will I know when to meet you?"

"You will know," Zoroaster said. "I will get word to you. No matter where you are. You will know."

"But what if—" Jarvey broke off, his mouth hanging open. Zoroaster was gone. He had not exactly vanished, had not faded away. It was as if he had been only a projected picture, and someone had switched the projector off.

Jarvey backed out from the shadows beneath the bridge. He wanted to be with someone he knew. He climbed the bank up to the bridge and set off for the Den. It was his only home now.

"We're movin'. Now," Betsy said grimly. "This place is too hot for us."

Jarvey groaned. He was hungry and his muscles ached from fatigue and effort. Everyone had turned up at the Den by twilight, and now Betsy walked back and forth, speaking in an angry voice. "There was too many tippers on the wharves today. Something got their suspicions up, and if that's happened, we've got to find another snug. I know one we can reach tonight, but we have to start now. Jarvey, get ready."

Jarvey took the Grimoire from its hiding place and tucked it inside his shirt.

Someone nudged Jarvey from behind. "That was too close, mate."

Jarvey wrinkled his nose at the blast of bad breath. It was Charley. "Yeah, it was," Jarvey whispered back.

"There's a rat here, you know, Jarv."

"What?" Jarvey knew there were real rats in Lunnon—some of the kids had talked about hard times when they had hunted down rats for food—but somehow he didn't think that was what Charley meant.

"A rat. Somebody peached, told them tippers we was going to be workin' the waterfront today. That's why so many of them was there waitin' for us. Didn't you think that was strange, like?"

"I didn't know what to think," Jarvey said. "I just wanted to get away from them."

"You watch Bets," Charley said in a low voice. "I think this might have been a put-up job. Like maybe she'd get herself caught, and you'd swap the book for her, or something."

Jarvey felt even colder. His throat tightened. He had thought of trading the book for his friends' freedom, but—Betsy?

Charley jerked his head toward Betsy, who was busy with the other kids. "Keep an eye out, is all. If there's a rat among us, just know you can never trust a rat."

"All right, then," Betsy was saying. "We'll split up. You leaders know where to take your groups. We'll take it slow. Charley, you'll take the first one, then Puddler will go, and last of all me. If it gets safe to join together again, I'll get word to Charley, and he'll see that Puddler hears. Ready to go, then?"

"Come with me," Charley suggested to Jarvey.

"He's with me," Betsy said sharply. "Get on with you now."

"Don't burst a blood vessel," Charley said easily. "Hi, you lot—with me. Come along, then."

Pattering feet in the twilight as Charley's group dropped down into the drain and scurried away. When their echoes had died, Betsy said, "Right, then. Puddler, you're next. Along with you, and remember to keep to the shadows."

Jarvey felt something scratchy in the neck of his shirt. He put a finger in and explored. He pulled out a card, though in the dimness he could not read it. Maybe Zoroaster's card, though he didn't remember keeping it. He stuck it into his pants pocket.

Puddler had been gone for ten minutes when Betsy spoke again: "Our turn. Let's hurry. There's the feel of rain, and I don't like wading through knee-deep water down there."

Jarvey fell into place right behind Betsy as they

scuttled down into the drain. He carried the book against his chest, under his shirt, and squirmed at the touch of its cover. It was hard to believe that the book wasn't alive, because the cover seemed to pulse, even to squirm, against his chest. He tried to ignore it. Betsy was in a hurry. They jogged through the dark, stooped over, breathing in the dank, stale air of the storm drains. They passed the grate where they usually emerged, made a turn, then another, until Jarvey felt completely lost. Still they hurried on, like a line of—well, of rats skittering through a tunnel.

Up on the surface the rain began. They couldn't hear it, but soon they splashed through an ankle-deep rivulet of cold running water. Jarvey grimaced. The streets in the Toffs' neighborhoods were always cleaned, but not in other places. Rotting garbage lay strewn in some streets until the rain washed it away. And when the water did sweep the filth away, it wound up here.

"Not much farther," gasped Betsy. "But I want to scout ahead. You lot stays here."

They milled uneasily in the rising water for a few minutes, and then they heard her voice again: "Right, come on. It's pouring up there, and we're going to get a dousing climbing out, but it can't be helped. Jarvey, I'll go first, and then you hand it to me."

"I can manage it," Jarvey said quickly.

"Suit yourself. Come on."

The grate was just over their heads. A rush of water spilled through it and splashed the floor of the drain under it. Two of the boys made a stirrup of their hands and hoisted Betsy up. She slipped the iron drain cover aside, then climbed out through the falling water. She reached an arm down on the dry side. "Come on, grab hold and I'll help you."

Jarvey turned his back on the rushing water, grabbed Betsy's outstretched hand, and felt the others boosting him as he kicked and hauled himself up. Betsy was strong, and she did more than her

share. Jarvey tried to keep himself curled over the Grimoire, protecting it.

He climbed up into dim light. "Where are we?"

"Courtyard. Back behind us is where some servants lives. Quiet."

When they were all up, Betsy led them to some protection from the spear-sharp rain, a carriage house. It had been left carelessly open, and they gratefully huddled inside, hearing the drumming of rain on its roof.

"Mill overseers live on this street," Betsy whispered. "They ain't so high-and-mighty as Toffs, but they ain't our friends either. I know this family pretty well. They have a daughter my age, and I've even talked to her now and again. She thinks I'm the daughter of a chief tipper—"

Somebody giggled, and Betsy hissed, "Stop! Quiet, now."

"Aw, Bets," someone else said. "In this rain they couldn't hear a brass band. We're safe enough."

Betsy ignored that. "We'll stay here a bit, see if the rain eases off. It generally does by midnight. Then we're not far from some places where we can hole up. Puddler and his bunch have gone to the safest snug, 'cause they're the youngest. Charley's takin' the others to the butcheries—I know, I know, it ain't the healthiest snug around, but Charley knows how to get 'em in and out safe. We're going to break up, so that each of us is in a different place, but we'll be close enough so we can get back together by night. All right?"

Jarvey heard a general, reluctant murmur of consent. His stomach felt fluttery. He hadn't been on his own since that first horrible night, weeks ago. And though Charley had warned him that being with the others didn't necessarily mean he was safe, he didn't like the thought of being on his own in Lunnon, especially not in a place so close to the Toffs.

The pounding rain slackened gradually, and

by midnight it had given way to a heavy, drifting drizzle, more of a choking fog than a real shower. They slunk out of their shelter and squelched along. Betsy sent one of the boys into an abandoned stable—"They sold their horse, and they ain't bought another for over a year, so it should be safe if you climb up into the hayloft and keep quiet by day." Another would hide in the attic of a small restaurant. "You can climb up onto the porch roof," Betsy whispered to him. "Then you'll find the ventilator cover's loose. Be sure to pull it back after you. They never come up there, but there's a lot of old pots and pans stacked about, so mind you don't blunder into them. Stay quiet through the day and go out after dark."

Then she led Jarvey for what felt like miles. "Saved the best for us," she muttered. "'Cept it's the most dangerous too. We're going to stay in a right snooty place, we are. Close to the palace itself."

"What?" Jarvey whispered.

"Look," Betsy said wearily, "you were right about the palace. You don't know how to use that book. I don't know. The only one that does is old Nibs. Somethin' in his house might hold the key, so we've got to go lookin' for it. If we're caught, we'll be—I don't know. Chopped up into pieces and stewed, maybe. But if we stay out dodgin' tippers long enough, you're going to be taken, and then what's the odds?"

"How far is it?"

"Not far."

They walked some more, and then Jarvey asked, "What is this place we're going to?"

"Palace has servants, right?" Betsy whispered back. "Some of them, the la-di-dah ones, lives right in the palace, but most don't, cleanin' maids and that. Well, within a short walk of the palace is a kind of flats block—you know what that is, a flats block?"

"What we call an apartment house," Jarvey said. "Yes, I know."

"Right. Well, this one has about a dozen flats

in it, for the women servants. Every flat has three girls in it. But it's like most buildings—it has an attic, and the attic is empty. And we can stay there because servant girls is superstitious, and from time to time they hear a ghost up there."

"What do you mean, a——"

"Ooooooooo," moaned Betsy, her voice rising and falling.

"Oh."

"Come on. Ain't no way up to the attic from the outside, though you can climb out onto the roof from there and get away in a pinch. Got to go in through the building before first light, when one of 'em goes to the pump to fetch water."

They crept through the night until at last they reached a two-storied house, dark and silent. Ahead of them, gas lights made ruddy wavering circles in the fog. "The palace gates," Betsy whispered. "Guards there, but what with the weather and the dark, they'll pay us no notice. Come with me."

The stone house lay surrounded by hedges, and Betsy led the way into a narrow clear space between wall and hedge. The front door was at the top of a short flight of six stone steps, and Betsy and Jarvey crouched beside these for what seemed like hours, until Jarvey's knees began to throb. The fog had just begun to turn a paler shade of gray when lights came on inside the house. A moment later, Jarvey heard the click of the front door being unlocked, and then two girls, each with a yoke over her neck from which dangled two big empty pails, came out, sniffing the morning air.

"Going to be a wet day," one of them observed.

"We'll have to hang the clothes inside, then," the other returned.

Chatting, the two of them clanked off into the gloom, and as soon as they had gone, Betsy tugged at Jarvey's sleeve. "Now."

They climbed over the step rail and ducked inside. The house was as silent as could be. Betsy led Jarvey up a dim stairway, illuminated only by a low gas night-light at each landing. The last stretch of stairs ended at a trapdoor in the ceiling. Betsy shoved at it, and it creaked open. She climbed through it, beckoning Jarvey to follow.

He pulled himself through, and together they let the trapdoor drop down silently. Jarvey fought an urge to sneeze. The air in the attic drifted thick with dust. "Don't move now," Betsy said. "Get into a comfortable position and stay that way until all the maids leave for the palace."

He stretched out, more or less, and soon dozed off. He didn't know how long he slept, but when Betsy shook him awake again, he could see. Thin daylight filtered in through ventilators in each gable of the steep roof. It didn't help much. Close to the trapdoor, a rampart of trunks and boxes stood, evidently hauled up to the attic in years past and then forgotten, for all of them wore furry coats of gray dust.

"They're out," Betsy said. "I think they've all gone. Sometimes one of them is sick and stays behind, and then you've got to be really quiet. Today, though, it sounds like they've all left for the palace. We'll hole up behind the trunks and things. I'll go down to their kitchens and slenk some food for us."

"Okay," agreed Jarvey. He stretched and then explored. If they had everything behind the trunks to themselves, they had most of the attic. It felt warm—warmer than the old Den in the alley, any-way—and seemed dry enough. Behind him, Betsy dropped through the trapdoor. Jarvey drew close enough to one of the big round ventilators to have a reasonable amount of daylight, and then he pulled out the Grimoire and studied its covers.

The way to find his parents, Zoroaster had said, lay in the Grimoire. He tugged at it, but it remained obstinately shut, as though the pages had been glued together. Jarvey took some minutes building up his nerve, then tapped the front cover with his finger and said, "Open!" in what he hoped was a commanding voice. Nothing happened. He took a deep breath and muttered, "I, Jarvis Midion, command you to open!"

The book seemed unimpressed.

Jarvey sighed and inspected the volume. The brass hinges gleamed dully against the pebbled, brownish red surface, and the brass catch could be flicked open easily enough. Still, regardless of what Zoroaster might have believed, the pages obstinately refused to open. Even for a Midion.

Clutching the book against his chest, his chin resting on the top edge, Jarvey thought about the weird moment when Siyamon Midion had given an order in a strange language. What had it been? Abracadabra, or something like that? Jarvey strained, but he could not quite bring back the strange syllables he had heard just before Zoroaster had barged in, yelling for him to beware the book. Jarvey could recall his own terror, the heart-stopping sensation of being turned inside out, of falling endlessly. He could see in his mind's eye long, crooked streaks of red and blue lightning. He could remember hearing shrieks and moans from the book's fluttering pages.

Not the words, though, not the spell that Siyamon had shouted just before the world had gone crazy. And if he could remember them, what then? He shuddered at the thought of the Grimoire opening once more, pulling him from Lunnon into some even worse place, if that were possible.

Zoroaster might have helped, but he had disappeared again, and Jarvey couldn't just wait around for him. There was only one other alternative. If he wanted to learn something about the magic that controlled the book, he had to find his way into the palace.

The trapdoor opened and closed, interrupting Jarvey's thoughts, and in a moment Betsy joined him, a look of triumph on her face. "Not too bad," she announced. "They keep a larder of food here for night meals, for most of them eat in the palace kitchens by day. I took a bit from here and a bit from there, and no one's likely to miss any of it. Cheese, biscuits, grapes, apples, even some chocolates. Help yourself."

They began to munch on the food. Jarvey tilted his head. "You're talking different," he said.

She shrugged. "On the street you learns to talk street talk, cully. Away from the street, you can speak more properly if you wish."

Jarvey didn't say anything, but he seemed to hear Charley's voice whispering inside his head: "Wonder what else she's been hidin' from you, mate."

Impulsively, Jarvey said, "Tell me more about your mother."

"Don't know much. I haven't seen her in ages, and I don't think I can find her, at least as long as old Nibs runs this town. What you and I have to do is take it away from him."

Jarvey shook his head. "Why did he make Lunnon in the first place?"

She laughed without really sounding amused. "I've had a lot of time to think about that. Well, for one thing, he's old, really old. In the year 1848, he would have been about seventy. Now you say that in the real world, the world where he came from, a hundred and sixty years or so have gone by. So he's two hundred and thirty, right? In real time, he'd be long dead by now. In book time, he stops aging. He stays the same as he was when he came into the book. So he made this place in order to live forever. And why did he make it with the Toffs and the rest of us? Why, cully, people like Tantalus Midion ain't happy lest they have a boot on some poor unfortunate's neck."

She leaned a little closer. "Listen, here's what I think. Tantalus couldn't make all of Lunnon. That's too big a magic even for him, even when he had the Grimoire. He could open the way to this place, but not create a city. So he found this world, saw it was the right proper sort of spot for what he

156

wanted, and started in on his plan. He began to bring people here. First some of the Toffs, men who didn't want to die and who took his way out of the real world."

"Magicians like him?"

"No, I don't think so. Least, nobody's ever seen anyone but old Nibs do magic in Lunnon. See, his Toffs can't do magic, but he can use 'em to drive the others. Then with the Toffs' help, old Tantalus kidnapped laborers, and maybe their wives and children. People to build, see? Lumber mills and brick mills and things, and then houses and places to make clothes and cook food and so on. And the children of those first laborers were born, and instead of staying babies, they grew up and became the next generation of poor folk and workers, and they had to be servants and slave in the mills. And old Nibs and the Toffs, why, they lorded it over all. Nibs is king here. He made Lunnon the way he remembered the old world, but put himself on top of the heap, like."

"But only the Toffs are happy. Everyone else—"

"Everyone else doesn't matter," she said flatly. "I doubt there's more than a thousand or two thousand like my mother. Transports, I mean. Everyone else was born here, and for us book time is real time."

Jarvey thought about that. "Look, I'm trying to find a way to open the Grimoire. But if I do, what happens?"

Betsy grinned. "Don't know. But I *think* what may happen is that you'll open the door back to your world from this side. If you do, then maybe we can send Nibs back to the real world, and he'd be stuck there, because he wouldn't have the book to get back to Lunnon."

Jarvey licked his lips. "Zoroaster seemed to think—he hinted that it might be the end of the world. The end of this world, anyway. Lunnon might disappear, everyone in it might die."

She shrugged. "What's the odds? Go on living like we do, like rats under their feet, or have it all over with and die quick and clean?" Her green eyes almost glowed in the faint light. "I'd sooner go quick than linger on in misery."

Something tickled Jarvey's leg, like an insect walking over his skin, and when he reached down to brush it off, he found the card he had fished out of his collar and shoved in his pocket. It had worked its way almost out, and when he looked at it, he saw tiny, spidery handwriting:

ESTELLA MAY BE FOUND IN MERCY PARK, AT THE CORNER OF FAULES AND MASON STREETS.

"What's that?" Bets asked.

Jarvey passed the card to her. "I don't know. I thought this belonged to Zoroaster, but—what's wrong?"

"Nothing." Betsy crumpled the card. "Just rubbish. Look, you need to get some rest. It's been a hard day." She made her way to the far side of the attic, where she sat with her back against a wall and her knees drawn up. Something about her posture warned Jarvey not to question her about the message.

Jarvey stretched out on the floor and tried to get comfortable, still wondering about the Grimoire and what he might be able to do if he opened it. If he sent Tantalus back, would the old man wind up in his own time, or in the twenty-first century? What would happen to Jarvey and his parents? He shivered at the thought of being thrust into the remote past, lost, still separated from his mom and dad.

"I want to go home," he whispered, so softly that not even Bets's sharp ears could have heard the small, forlorn sound. "I just want to go home."

Maybe Bets preferred a quick, clean end. Jarvey wanted life. Not only for himself, but also for his mother and his father.

CHAPTER 9
New Shirts

*T*hey hid in the attic for three days. By daylight they ate and slept, and some of Jarvey's strength returned as the aches and bruises healed themselves. Jarvey sneaked down into the stairwell after the first day and spent hours standing at a narrow window looking out toward the palace. He saw a high brick wall, with guard boxes on either side of a barred iron gate. Inside the boxes stood two unsmiling men at all times, beefy fellows who looked dangerous. That was where he and Zoroaster had emerged when Jarvey first arrived.

From the window's height, Jarvey could see a broad green lawn shaded by scattered trees, and beyond them a boxy stone house with arched windows and white shutters a hundred yards or so inside the gate. As far as he could see, the brick wall surrounded the grounds.

Sometimes people got in, though. In the mornings, small carts loaded with food rumbled up, and the guards would unlock the gate. The carts took a route that Jarvey couldn't quite see, a pathway around the inside of the wall, toward the back of the house. Once in a while a tipper, carrying a stack of papers, would approach and salute the men. They usually let the tipper inside, though once in a while a male servant dressed in black would come down from the house and take the papers through the iron bars instead.

Servants got in, of course. One evening Tantalus must have thrown a party. In the dim twilight, the house blazed with light, and twenty men and women, dressed as servants, walked up to the gate and were admitted. Before long, Toff carriages rolled up to the gates and let people out. Most were horse-drawn, but a few were pulled by teams of boys, dressed in silk uniforms but whipped like animals. That night the women who lived in the house were very late coming home, and the next day on a food raid Betsy was able to snare some delicious cake and some other tidbits.

On the first day, Betsy sneaked out and was gone for hours, returning silent and pale. When she remained withdrawn for hours, he began to worry. But whenever he asked, "Bets, is something wrong?" she would just shake her head and look away. Jarvey wondered where she had gone and what had happened, but if she didn't want to talk about it, he felt that prying would be wrong. Still, he woke at least once to the sound of Betsy's quiet sobbing. The sense that something bad had happened to her just added to Jarvey's uneasiness and to his growing sense that he had to find a way to get into the palace.

Toward the end of the third day, Jarvey made up

his mind. He told Betsy, "I'm going to try to get into the palace somehow. I'll hide the book up here. If I get caught, at least old Tantalus won't get his hands on that."

"You think you're ready for this?" Betsy asked.

Jarvey shook his head. "No. I'm not. But I can't think of any other way of trying to find my mom and dad. I'll never be ready, but I'm going to have to try."

"Luck, then," Betsy said. "I'll watch out for you. If you need help and you can think of any way to get word to me——"

"You'll hear from me," Jarvey said with a sick smile.

He left the next morning, as two girls went out for water. Jarvey had made what plans he could think of. One thing he had to have was different clothes. In Lunnon, you were a Toff, a servant, or one of the working poor. He wore the clothes of a poor kid, and he needed to look like a servant of some kind, at least a low-level servant. If you had a master, people let you alone.

He hid out for most of the day, finding a safe spot in a woodshed a mile or so from the palace. When the brassy light of the sky faded to twilight, he ventured out.

This part of Lunnon was a district of small servant cottages with meager yards and tiny back gardens. As night came on, weary men and women plodded home, and soon the smell of frying fish and stewing cabbage began to drift out on the air. Jarvey heard music from some of the houses, plaintive violins and tinkling pianos. None of it sounded cheerful. Now and then he risked a glance through a window, seeing men in their shirtsleeves and women in aprons settling down at tables, their faces looking strained and weary. In some of the houses children sat at the tables too.

A little farther, and Jarvey found a darkened street of shops: shoes, iron goods, kitchen things.

And a shop that sold used clothing. It was locked tight, though. He crept in the tight space beneath the front steps of the shop and settled in for a restless night.

With the coming of daylight, he crawled out again and loitered around until an old man and old woman unlocked the shop. He didn't dare go inside until he was sure they were busy somewhere in the back. Then he hastily ducked through the door, catching his breath when a bell tinkled and the old woman called, "I'll be with you in a minute, dearie!"

A wilderness of racks surrounded him, and from them hung clothes in all sizes. Against one wall he saw a long shelf piled high with stockings and underwear, and under it stacks of boot and shoe boxes. Jarvey scrambled under the shelf, worming his way into a narrow space between the shoe boxes and the wall. Just as he did, the bell rang again, and he heard footsteps hurrying from the back of the store. The old woman said, "Well, Mrs. McCarty, and I hope I see you the same."

"Pretty well, dearie, I thank you," said another woman's voice. "I'm in need of a black frock, Mrs. Shandy, if you've one that's not too dear. My master wants me to wait on his son and daughter-in-law next week, and I've nothing suitable to wear as a lady's maid, me so long in the kitchen and all."

"I think we can fit you right up, Mrs. McCarty. Come with me, dear, and we'll see what we have."

From then on Jarvey lay still and listened to a steady stream of customers, some buying and some selling. At long last, he heard the two elderly shop owners talking to each other.

The man said, "Well, Mrs. Shandy, not such a bad day."

"No, Mr. Shandy, but if we don't sell more than we buy, we're in for trouble."

"Never fear, Mrs. Shandy. We buy cheap and we

sell dear, and that's the way to make the world go around."

"Have you locked up the back, dear?"

"I have, my pet. Now, it's likely we'll have no more customers today, so what say you to closing early and having a pint at the public house before curfew?"

"I say a pint would be welcome, Mr. Shandy."

The old couple both chuckled at that, and soon Jarvey heard the front door close and a key turn in the lock. He waited a few minutes more and then slipped out of his hiding place.

He explored the dim shop and found in the back a bathroom with running water. Trickling water, anyway. He closed the door and turned up a small gas lamp. He blinked into a bleary, corroded mirror hanging over a cumbersome, rusty sink.

His face was a mess. He couldn't remember the last time he'd washed. Probably his plunge into the river, if you could call that washing. His rusty brown hair was so dirty that it lacked the usual odd highlights, and it was too long, longer than he liked it, hanging over his ears and down low on the back of his neck.

He needed that change of clothes. Keeping to the back of the store, Jarvey hunted through the racks for something he could wear. Finally he found a white shirt, gray vest and jacket, and short black trousers. He turned up some thick white stockings and a pair of shoes that were tight, but he thought he could stand them.

Then he returned to the little bathroom and gave himself as much of a bath as he could with just a sink, a bar of coarse brown soap, and a dribble of cold water. When his reflection in the mirror looked clean, or anyway cleaner, he got into the clothes. They felt weird, like a Halloween costume. The shoes pinched his feet, and the vest was too loose, but otherwise he looked the part of a houseboy or errand-runner. He hoped.

He buried his old clothes at the bottom of a rag bin. When he turned the gas light down and opened the bathroom door, Jarvey realized that night had fallen. He stood in the dark store, debating with himself. He could find a way out now, but that meant spending another night dodging the Mill Press and tippers. But if he stayed in the store, he'd have difficulty slipping out after the Shandys arrived. And he was very hungry.

Jarvey felt his way to a closed door, presumably the door to the office. It was locked. He rattled the door, but had no way of opening it.

A gleam of light shone through the front window, and Jarvey dropped to the floor, lying on his stomach. The light flickered as someone—probably a tipper with a dark lantern, a kind of oil-burning flashlight—tried the front door, found it locked, and moved on. Jarvey lay still for another full minute. He reached out to push himself up, and his hand hit the door.

Which moved.

Exploring by feel, Jarvey finally understood what had happened. The office door had a pet flap in it. Maybe the Shandys had once owned a cat or a guard dog that slept in the office. He didn't think one was in the shop now. He hadn't heard any sign of a pet all day long, anyway. He could get his head and one arm through the flap. Maybe with a little squirming—

He wormed through the opening and stood up, feeling his way. Another gas jet burned low and blue on the wall. He cautiously eased it up, saw that the cubicle had no windows, and then turned the gas up full. Against one wall of the little office stood a long, scarred, chipped desk, taking up most of the space. A squat iron safe was against the opposite wall, and next to it a narrow door. A litter of papers covered the desk, most of them scrawled bills and invoices.

Jarvey searched for something useful and found

a few crusts of bread left over from sandwiches. A withered apple was on one corner of the desk. The scraps were barely enough to remind his stomach that he was hungry. When he had eaten, Jarvey opened the narrow door next to the safe and saw a sort of closet stacked with new-looking boxes. One of them had a stenciled legend on its visible side: OLDCASTLE AND SON, TAILORS. It was the right size for a jacket or a half-dozen shirts, and it gave Jarvey an idea. He took it—it was empty—and soon had it stuffed with his old clothes. He found twine and tied the package securely.

Jarvey waited until almost dawn before he dared to go to the front of the shop and examine the door. He could unlock it from the inside—the deadbolt had a twist latch—but he couldn't relock it. Jarvey bit his lip and decided to risk it. The Shandys were old, and they had gone to a public house for ale or beer before going home. Maybe the old man would think he'd just forgotten to lock up. It wasn't likely either of them would realize that they'd been robbed. The clothes Jarvey had taken came from scattered racks, and with the thousands of articles of clothing crammed into the little store, it would be all but impossible to tell that a few odds and ends had vanished.

He stepped out into a clammy, foggy early morning. A few people were stirring about already as he walked up the street. In a kind of square, a lot of them had gathered at a pump, where they gossiped as they filled buckets. A man noticed Jarvey staring at the crowd. "What's your trouble, young'un?" he asked.

Jarvey blinked, then tested his ability to sound English: "Please, sir, I'm a new errand boy at Oldcastle's, and I've a half-dozen shirts for the palace."

"Lord love you," a woman said with a chuckle. "Afraid to go there, are you? If you've business there, they'll not hurt you. But you're early, you know. Best wait until full day to make your delivery."

"Don't look for no tip, neither," another man advised. "Likely if you ask at the front gate, they'll send you around to the back, anyway, so you'd best go round there to begin with. Nip in, nip out, and don't make no trouble."

"Aye, or you'll find yourself in the mills," the first man said.

"Thank you."

The woman tilted her head. "You eat yet, lad?"

"No, I haven't. These shirts were promised for yesterday, but Mr. Oldcastle didn't get them finished until after dark, and I was afraid to take the package then."

"Wise you were. Here, I've drawn my water. Come along with me and carry it for me, and you can have a bite of breakfast with my two. They're not old enough for service yet, but 'twill do them good to see a young fellow already trusted with shirts for the palace."

With his box clutched under his left arm, Jarvey

lugged the heavy pail of water in his right hand. The family's name was Broad, and they lived up to it: Mrs. Broad was chunky and smiling, with a red berry face always in motion. Mr. Broad was grave and heavyset—"Under-butler to Lord Wainford," Mrs. Broad said in tones of pride. The little Broads were a girl, six, and a boy, four, round butterballs with wide eyes. Jarvey tried to remember his manners as he sat at the table and had a fried egg, thick bacon, toast, marmalade, and cool milk. He couldn't remember the last time he had eaten with a knife and fork.

Mr. Broad gave his wife a peck on the cheek and then went off to work. Jarvey helped her clear the table, while she chattered away about how his mum and dad must be proud of him, getting a job with the Oldcastles, the tailors the Toffs always liked to use. Jarvey blushed. She was a nice woman, and he felt strange lying to her.

After offering his thanks to Mrs. Broad, Jarvey

escaped finally when day was bright in the streets. With his package under his arm, he made his way toward the palace, wondering if Betsy was still in the snug above the block of flats. He hoped she would be at the stairway window watching him, for he felt lonely and deserted.

Giving the front gate of the palace a wide berth, Jarvey followed the street as it curved off to the right. The palace stood alone in its own green square of land. The cottages of the servants ended outside the front wall, and to either side and the back he saw only rolling green hills and trees—the palace park, he supposed, off-limits to everyone but Tantalus Midion and his guests. He walked close to the brick wall, which went on for nearly a quarter of a mile before he came to the back corner. Then he found the back guard-houses, identical to the front ones, with identically tough-looking men in both of them. Feeling shaky, he approached one and said, "I beg your pardon, sir, but I've this parcel to deliver to the palace."

The guard stared at him. "Where from?"

"From Oldcastle's, sir." Jarvey held it up so the guard could see the label. "New shirts, sir."

"All right. In with you. Servants' door is at the end of the lane. Stay on the lane, mind, or the dogs might rip you up."

"Thank you, sir."

The guard unlocked the gate and waved Jarvey through. The lane was a strip of lawn, bordered on either side by a tall wrought-iron fence. Jarvey had taken no more than a dozen steps when he heard a snarling and the scrabble of paws. Two short-haired brown dogs, hounds that came nearly up to his waist, thrust their muzzles through the fence and snuffled, growling at him, the fur on their necks and shoulders bristling.

They didn't bark at all. The sounds they made were worse, low and guttural, as if they wanted to shred him to bite-size morsels and gulp them down. They paced him all the way down the lane and up to the big, square stone house.

As he neared the palace, Jarvey saw something that might prove useful later on. Off to his right, an old tree grew close to the wall, one sturdy limb actually touching the top row of bricks. Next to it was another tree, with its limbs interlacing with the first. If a person could climb up onto the wall and into the tree, he just might be able to creep along through the branches until he reached the protection of the lane. Then he could drop down safely and be inside the palace grounds.

Except that the dogs would bark at him, and people would investigate and catch him if he tried that.

The rumble of the dogs grew louder as Jarvey came up to the green-painted back door of the palace. A ponderous iron knocker in the shape of a lion's head gripping a huge iron ring in its jaws hung there. Jarvey lifted it and let it fall.

A moment later, a young woman opened the door. "Yes, boy?"

"A package for Mr. Robinson, from Oldcastle's," Jarvey said, remembering Charley's technique.

The young woman, who wore a white blouse and a gray skirt, frowned. "Robinson? Robinson? Old Bill, the chamberlain? I suppose you'd better take them to him, then. Down the hall to the end, then left, then up the stair, then right, and his is the third room on the left. If he's not in, leave it outside his door."

"Thank you, miss."

"Mind you watch your step," she said.

"Yes, miss."

The kitchen must be somewhere nearby, Jarvey thought, from the smell of cooking. He walked slowly down the hall, stepping out of the way when servants bustled past him. They didn't give him a second look. Too many servants, he decided, and he seemed to have some purpose, walking along with his package tucked under his arm.

He reached the end of the hall. Before him were

two great arched doors, the wood carved to repre-
sent animal heads: lions, elephants, water buffalo,
other creatures. Before he could turn toward the
stairway, both doors opened suddenly. A tall man
stood there for a moment, staring at Jarvey.

Jarvey's heart nearly popped out of his mouth.
He knew the face.

It was a cruel face, thin and pale. A pink scar zig-
zagged from the forehead down over the blind right
eye. From a deep, dark socket, the left eye glared at
him.

It was the tipper who had very nearly caught him
at the river.

CHAPTER 10
In the Grip of the Hawk

"Who's that?" The querulous, old-man's voice came from behind the one-eyed tipper. "Hawk, who is that?"

The thin, black-clad tipper stepped aside. "An errand lad, my lord."

Jarvey swallowed. Tantalus Midion, his blue eyes piercing beneath shaggy white brows, glowered in the doorway. Jarvey caught his breath. If old Midion could really sense magic, would he sense Jarvey's art? Midion barked, "Boy, what are you doing here?"

Jarvey's voice caught in his throat. "I, uh, some shirts here to—to go back to Oldcastle's for mending, sir."

"Bah! Sell 'em to a rag shop."

"Y-yes, sir. Thank you, sir."

The tipper shot out his hand and grabbed Jarvey's shoulder. "Do you not know whom you're addressing, snipe? Say 'my lord' to your betters!"

"Yes, my lord. Forgive me, my lord. I never saw you before, my lord."

"Wait a bit," old Tantalus growled with a wave of his hand. "Hawk, Oldcastle's is in Holofernes Street. This errand lad can save you a trip. Give him the message."

"Are you sure, my lord?" The tipper's voice grated. "It is an important message."

"He'll see it there safe if he knows what's good for him. The Oldcastles know where their loyalty lies, and they have whips for dealing with messengers whose speed displeases me." Old Midion's lips spread in an evil smile. "But you are young and strong, my lad. No doubt you are fleet of foot as well. Give him the envelope, Mr. Hawk."

Mr. Hawk's one eye, a strange shade of yellow-brown, glared at Jarvey as the man reached into his leather tunic and produced a heavy tan envelope. He held it out. "To go to the Holofernes Street police station, to be handed to the sergeant of the watch. You are to wait upon his reply and bring it here at a run—at a run, mind you."

Jarvey reached a shaking hand for the envelope, but before his fingers could close on it, Mr. Hawk twitched it back. "Repeat your orders, errand boy, to make sure you understand them."

In a quick, breathless voice, Jarvey said, "Take the message to the watch sergeant at the Holofernes Street police station. Wait for a reply and bring it back quickly."

For a frozen moment Mr. Hawk stood frowning at him, as if vaguely dissatisfied. Then, slowly, he lowered the envelope so that Jarvey could take it. "Thank you, sir," Jarvey said, and he turned and hurried out as fast as he could.

The guard at the gate stared at him. "Why are

you bringing that box back, then?" he demanded.

"Other shirts, need mending," Jarvey said. He held up the envelope. "And Mr. Hawk gave me this to deliver."

Without another word, the guard opened the gate and let him out. Jarvey ran along the wall, turned the corner, and ducked out of sight. Holofernes Street? He'd never heard of it. But if he could deliver the letter and return with a reply, at least that would get him back into the palace. Jarvey fell into a jog, and when he reached the fountain, an idea struck him. He made his way to the Broad family's house and rapped on the door.

Red-faced Mrs. Broad answered his knock, her arms dusted with flour and her nose smudged with what looked like butter. "Why, what's the trouble?" she asked, her eyebrows arched in surprise. "Wouldn't they let you in the palace, dear?"

"Oh, Mrs. Broad," Jarvey said, "I'm in terrible trouble. I'm to take this note to the Holofernes

Street tippers' station, and this is my first day as an errand boy, and I don't know where that is!"

Mrs. Broad's faced crinkled in puzzlement. "Don't know that? Why, it's not far past Oldcastle's, love. Look, the quickest way is down Palace Street here across the arched bridge, then left onto Lime Street, and that will run into Holofernes. Just turn left again there, and you'll find your bearings right enough. After you pass Oldcastle's, just straight on for a quarter mile, and there you are."

"Thank you!" Jarvey called back over his shoulder, because he was already off at a trot.

The arched bridge led not across a river, but over a green parklike stretch of lawn and trees where a dozen Toffs strolled and chatted. Lime Street was a row of shops, and Holofernes a broad cobbled street lined with better shops and thick with Toffs. Jarvey saw the tailor shop of Oldcastle and Son, a grand building with a gilded hanging sign, and he hurried past it before someone could notice his package and ask him about it.

He came to a rubbish bin and disposed of the box of rags. Then he examined the envelope. It had not been carefully sealed. A round blob of wax over the point of the flap held it loosely closed, but a little pressure of his thumbnail would, yes, pop it free. Jarvey darted his eyes around, but Toffs never noticed errand boys. He slipped a single sheet of paper from the envelope and unfolded it.

The handwriting was old-fashioned and looping, but he could read it clearly enough:

> To Sergeant Wilkes:
>   His High Honor, the Lord
> Mayor, directs and charges you:
>   Our informer has sworn that
> a boy named Jarvis Green is
> a danger to our good interests.
> He is about twelve, with reddish

brown hair, and an odd manner of speaking. His eyes are blue. If found, care is to be taken not to harm him before he can be turned over to the palace for the question direct. Particular care is to be taken to secure him and all his possessions, as one of these may be of some interest.

The boy is believed to be in company with a gang of street urchins led by the girl called Betsy. You are directed and commanded to make a particular search for any members of this gang, with an eye to capturing the boy Jarvis Green. You may use methods of pain, but take care not to damage the children so much that they cannot give us information.

Jarvis Green is believed to have been in communication with Lord Zoroaster, who has been decreed a traitor against the interests of His Most High Excellency Tantalus Midion. The palace wishes to locate and capture Lord Zoroaster, as you know, but you are directed not to question the boy regarding Lord Zoroaster's whereabouts. I shall attend to that questioning myself.

I charge you to carry out these orders, standing to account for any failure at your own peril.

–Standridge Hawk
Captain, City Constabulary

Jarvey refolded the paper and tucked it back into the envelope. He pressed the blob of wax hard, and it adhered almost as well as it had before he had pried it loose. Well, he thought, Hawk wasn't as sharp as he might have been. He'd written the description, but he'd looked right at Jarvey without recognizing him.

Of course, Jarvey thought bitterly. A street urchin wore rags, and an errand boy wore a kind of uniform. He hesitated for only a moment, then jogged on. He had to get back into the palace. No sign marked the police station, but a uniformed tipper stood beside the door.

Jarvey hurried up to him. "Message for the watch sergeant, from Captain Hawk."

The man jerked his thumb over his shoulder. "Sergeant Wilkes you're wanting. Straight in with you."

Jarvey pushed through the door. Five or six tippers looked up in idle curiosity. "Sergeant Wilkes?" Jarvey asked.

"That's me, boy," a fattish, balding man said.

"Message for you, sir, and I'm to wait for a reply."

Wilkes took the envelope, ripped it open, and

read the letter. "Another note about those blasted young'uns. All right, let me tell old One-Eye that we're pursuing all leads, making inquiries, the lot." He folded himself into a chair at a green-topped table, reached for a sheet of paper and a steel pen, and laboriously scrawled a response. He blotted this, looked up keenly and asked, "Can't read, can you?"

"Me, sir? No, sir," Jarvey lied.

"Won't bother sealing it then. Back to old Hawk with you then, and take it at a run if you want him to leave you with a whole skin. Impatient man, our Captain Hawk."

"Yes, sir."

The scrawled reply told Jarvey nothing that the sergeant had not said aloud, except that it noted that Betsy's full name was probably Elizabeth Dare.

Charley had been right. Some rat had been talking to the tippers.

Jarvey didn't have time to wonder who the rat might be. He had other, more immediate worries.

CHAPTER 11
The Wolf's Lair

Jarvey was streaming with sweat by the time he reached the palace. He gasped up to the nearest gate guard and said, "Message from the Holofernes police station for Captain Hawk. Will you take it?"

"Not me, snipe," the guard said with a wicked grin. He unlocked the front gate. "In with you, and nip to the back. Careful of the dogs!"

Jarvey followed the path around the house to the back door, accompanied by the two growling dogs. Again he lifted the heavy knocker, and another servant admitted him. Jarvey followed him down the hall, through the big carved double doors, into a wide parlor, almost big enough to be a dance floor. It had a high, domed ceiling, and halfway up, a railed gallery ran around three of the walls. Beneath that, in the shadows, many dark wooden doors pierced the walls to left and right, and the servant led Jarvey to one of these. He tapped respectfully, and Captain Hawk opened the door. "In you go," whispered the servant, giving Jarvey a shove in the small of his back.

"Your answer, sir, from the sergeant," Jarvey said. He could not stop his heart from hammering at the foreboding one-eyed stare.

Hawk twitched the paper from Jarvey's hand with a delicate move of his fingers and said, "Come with me."

He led Jarvey down a familiar arched hallway and through another door. It opened into the library, this time bright with daylight streaming through a wall that was almost all windows. It looked different from the library that Jarvey had seen in Siyamon Midion's house—that room had had no windows at all, just floor-to-ceiling shelves of crumbling, ancient books.

Tantalus Midion sat in a tall chair, bent over a huge volume resting on his desk. He glanced up as they came in. "What now?"

"The answer from the station, my lord." Hawk gave the old man the folded paper.

Midion read it, his shaggy brows coming down in a fierce scowl. "What's this? 'An informer has told us the girl Betsy's name is Elizabeth Dare'!" He chuckled in a nasty way. "Well, well, I think we shall be all right, then, in time. Captain, make sure your men do not bungle this. It is of capital importance, I tell you. For weeks now I have known that something is not quite right, something in the very fabric of the city. This Green boy seems to be the key to it all. Fetch him to me, and soon, or I'll have your skin."

"We shall do everything in our power, my lord," Hawk said quietly.

Jarvey, without being obvious about it, gazed at the two walls of bookshelves on either side of the room. Volumes tall and short, fat and thin, jammed the shelves. Maybe one of them could tell him—

"Any further orders, my lord?" Hawk asked as Midion turned back to his book.

"Eh? No, no. Give the lad a copper or two and kick him on his way."

The hard hand of Hawk closed on Jarvey's shoulder, turned him around, and marched him out of the room. "Here," he said, and dropped four big coins, thin copper pieces with Tantalus Midion's face engraved on them, into Jarvey's hand. "Now back to your business. Next time you're sent to the palace, take care not to be seen by his lordship. He does not like to bother with servants." Unsmiling, Hawk added, "He could boil the flesh off your bones with a word, or turn you into something nasty."

"Y-yes, sir," Jarvey said. "May I go, sir?"

Hawk waved a long, bony hand toward the door,

threw back the tails of his black coat, and sat at a table spread with sheets of handwritten notes. He did not look up as Jarvey let himself out into the big room.

Jarvey left by the back door, went down the lane and around to the front, and headed for the block of flats where Betsy waited in the attic.

Since he wore the uniform of an errand boy, he chanced walking up to the front door and banging on it. If someone answered, he would ask directions. If the house was empty except for Betsy, maybe she would creep out onto the stairway and peek down from the front window. He knocked loudly, then stood back so she could see him.

Nothing happened. He tried again, without success, and then gave up. He'd have to wait until dark.

Jarvey loitered around, moving when anyone seemed to notice him, walking fast and with his head down, as if he had an urgent message to deliver. His stomach began to growl, and he found a stall selling fried fish. "How much?" he asked.

"One for a copper, three for two," the woman at the counter told him, and he gave up two of his copper coins in exchange for three hot fillets of fish. He wolfed these down, got a drink at the pump, and so made it through the day. Fog rose with the coming of night, dense and clinging. The chattering servants came home in a long, straggling line, and one of them, a plump, middle-aged woman, unlocked the front door. She stood as the others filed in, asking irritably, "Where's Alice and Penelope, then?"

"Late, as usual," one of the women said with a laugh. "I think our Alice is chatting with Mr. Blake, the groom, and Penelope will be there as chaperone."

"I'll leave the door unlocked for them," the older woman grumbled. "If that girl is going to marry, I wish she'd marry and have done with it!" The door closed on her quarreling voice.

Jarvey had been hiding behind the hedge bordering the front of the house. He slipped out, opened the front door slowly, slowly, allowing no creak, and then silently stepped inside. He heard voices down the hall to his left, more, fainter ones from upstairs, but he risked tiptoeing up the stairway. He took off his shoes before he reached the second landing, then hurried up past a hallway where clusters of women still stood chatting. Up to the top of the stair, through the trapdoor, and then as he was closing the trap, it slipped and swung down with a muffled thud.

"There's the ghost!" one of the women cried from below. She did not seem particularly frightened.

"Maybe Alice will come home and marry it," another one said, to a general laugh.

Jarvey breathed in relief. "Betsy?" he whispered as loudly as he dared. "Bets?"

No answer. Daylight was long gone, and the enveloping fog cut off any glimmer of gas light from the ventilators. The attic lay in absolute darkness. Jarvey slowly, carefully, groped his way behind the barrier of trunks and boxes. "Betsy!" His whisper became more urgent.

She wasn't there. Worse, he could not find the Grimoire. Feeling as if his world were on the verge of ending, Jarvey curled up and tried to rest. What if Charley had been right? He had warned Jarvey not to trust Betsy.

And if Betsy were the informer—if she had turned the Grimoire over to Hawk, or worse, to Midion—he couldn't even think about that.

If she had, his world had ended, and he was stuck here forever.

CHAPTER 12
Fighting the Odds

*B*etsy did not return over the next days. Though he was nearly frantic over the loss of the Grimoire, Jarvey didn't know where she had gone or how to reach her. He spent the time either sleeping in the attic or slinking through the streets, stealing food whenever he could. He had found a butcher's shop not far from the local pump, and he slenked odds and ends of raw meat from their refuse bin, but not for himself.

He had found a way inside the brick wall, the route he had spied on his first visit. The old oak tree near the wall drooped a branch down just low enough for him to scramble up, when it was dark enough for him to get in without being spotted. He could drop into the lane between the wall and the wrought-iron fence from there.

The two dogs must have been kept starved. They snarled and threatened him—until he began to toss them tidbits of raw meat. The first night they gobbled the meat, then growled and muttered. He sat in the tree until the dogs barked, then dropped back over the wall to safety. The same thing happened the second night, and the third, but then the dogs came running over not with rumbles of anger, but whimpers of anticipation. Jarvey found he could crouch in the dark and extend the meat to them. They let him ruffle their ears and even tried to stick their snouts through the fence to lick his face. "Good old boys, good old boys," he said in a soft voice. "Hungry, weren't you, guys?"

When a week had passed, Jarvey was sure the dogs knew him and would not tear him limb from limb if he had to get into the palace grounds by way of the tree. Well—*reasonably* sure.

A day came when he heard the maidservants in the flats eagerly chattering about their holiday—"A whole week, fancy!" one of them said. Jarvey listened hard, learning that Midion was planning to be away in the country, taking some of his chief advisors with him to have a governmental conference.

That night he slipped away from the apartment house and climbed up into the oak tree. The big stone house lay in quiet and darkness. Below the tree, the two dogs circled, whimpering and whining. Jarvey crouched in the branches, but he knew the dark house was bound to be locked up, and at last he dropped back over the wall, not sure what to do.

He no longer had the Grimoire, but he did have the art. Or sometimes he had it. Jarvey thought it over. Siyamon Midion had seemed to say that if someone had even "wild art," he could be trained to use it. But how did you train to use magic? If there were how-to books, the one place, the only place he could find them in Lunnon had to be in old Tantalus Midion's library. And maybe—he hated to think it, but the thought would not go away— maybe if Betsy had betrayed him, the Grimoire was kept inside the library too. The thought of sneaking back into Bywater House, into the library where he and his parents had been tricked, made him feel sick, and yet he could think of nothing else.

His errand-boy clothes were beginning to look shabby and dirty, and he no longer dared to show himself boldly on the streets. Jarvey had hoped to do this on his own, no longer trusting even Betsy. He had to face facts: He needed help. He needed the Free Folk.

The next day he went hunting. No one was in the old Den in the alley, and he wasn't even sure he could find the basement where he'd first met Betsy and the others. He remembered Charley's bunch had been sent to the butcheries. On a rough, narrow street called the Shambles, he found big butchers' shops where animals were slaughtered and their meat dressed. At one end of the street stood dozens of ramshackle stalls, where the tougher, less palatable cuts were sold to the poor. Jarvey hung around these, keeping an eye open.

He was almost ready to give up after two days of this when a group of three boys boiled out of a shop doorway and pelted around the corner. He recognized two of them, and one was Charley.

They had a good start, but desperation gave Jarvey an extra burst of speed. He ran as if he were trying to steal second in the last inning of a close game. Charley's head swung around, his eyes narrow, as he heard Jarvey's footsteps, and a broad brown-toothed grin spread itself across his grimy face. "Hold up, you two," he said, tossing his head to get his black hair out of his face. "Here's a turn-up! Old Jarvey Green! What cheer, Jarv?"

"I need some help," Jarvey gasped as he broke out of his sprint. "Listen, where's Bets?"

Charley frowned and scratched his head. "Dunno, mate. Dropped out o' sight, she has. Run into Puddler some time back, he said he seen her talkin' to a Toff near the palace, if that's any help."

Jarvey felt his heart sink. Betsy had kept the Grimoire. If she had taken it to the palace—

"You were right," he told Charley. "There's a rat. Listen." He hastily filled Charley in on what he had learned running errands for Captain Hawk. "So they're looking for us," he finished. "And they know Bets by name. Elizabeth Dare, the note said."

"Go on!" said one of the other boys, one Jarvey vaguely remembered as Bumper. "That's the same as—"

"Shut it," Charley said in a low voice. "Come on."

They went down to the river, where Charley made sure the coast was clear before leading the way into a boathouse built onto a wharf. The light inside was strange, cool and green, with ripples from the water crawling over the walls and ceiling. Once they were inside, they all sat on the edge of the wharf, dangling their feet. "Listen," Charley said, sounding reluctant. "I dunno if this is worth it or not to say, but I never knew Betsy's last name before. Dare? You sure it was Dare, mate?"

"Yeah," Jarvey said. "So what?"

Charley ran a brown hand though his mop of hair. "Well, then, it's—I dunno. Jarv, before old Nibs caught him stealin' and had him hung, Fortner Dare was captain of the watch. Head tipper, same as like Hawk is now."

Jarvey felt ice in his chest. "A tipper? Betsy's dad, you think?"

"Dunno what to think," muttered Charley. "But Dare ain't a common name. One of the Firsts was Fortner Dare. He couldn't die here, not naturally died. He had to be hung, didn't he? But whether he was Bets's dad or not, well, I dunno, mate."

Jarvey sat silent for long moments. Then Charley slapped him on the back. "Buck up, though. Tell you what: If you can get yourself up *to* the palace without bein' caught, I'll wager you I can get you *in*."

From somewhere in his rags he produced a metal ring of what looked like spikes and L-shaped rods of metal. "Lockpicks, mate. For gettin' in where nobody wants you. And if you're caught with lockpicks on you, mind, it ain't the mills for you. It's—" He drew his finger across his throat and made a horrible gurgling sound. "It's good-bye and farewell to your noggin, mate. It's a hangin' offense."

Jarvey had never studied anything in school as hard as he studied becoming a burglar. For two days Charley instructed him, letting him work on a wide sampling of locks that he had squirreled away in one of the hideouts. Jarvey learned how to feel for the tumblers inside the lock, how to ease them up and keep them up one at a time, until even the heaviest lock would spring open. Over and over they practiced, until Jarvey's knuckles ached and blisters stood on his thumb and forefinger from the effort. Finally, Charley said, "That's all I can teach you, mate. So are you willin' to risk the drop, then? You really goin' to do it, fighting the odds?"

"I don't want to," Jarvey confessed. "But I have to." He licked his dry lips. "Will you—Charley, will you come with me?"

Charley gave him his stained grin. "Nah, mate, only get you caught if I did. This here's a one-man job, see? Them dogs may wag their tails and turn over on their backs to see you, but they'd have my bleedin' leg off if I came along. My bunch might kind of stroll around, though, keep the guards' attention on us, like. Best we can do, mate."

So it was settled. The next day brought the worst fog yet. While the others went out gathering food and some bones for the dogs, Jarvey practiced with the lockpicks over and over. Night came on with a slow fading of the light, the fog still dense, nearly impenetrable. All the better.

They made their way through the dark streets, and Jarvey felt grateful for Charley's knowledge of Lunnon. In the fog, he would have lost himself after the first hundred feet. He carried the picks and a lumpy parcel of bones and meat, bribes for the watchdogs.

It must have been nearly midnight when they reached the brick wall. "Luck, mate," Charley whispered, slapping Jarvey's shoulder. "Sing out if you find yourself in trouble, and we'll do what we can."

With dread in every move, Jarvey made his way to the overhanging branch, by feel, not by vision, for everything was pitch black. Finally his stretched-out hands brushed the hanging twigs, and he hauled himself up into the tree. He made his way to the trunk and swung down. He would drop into the yard, not the lane, from there, and if the dogs had forgotten him—well, old Tantalus wouldn't have anything more to worry about.

Jarvey closed his eyes and let go. His heels hit the soft lawn with a thump, and he sat down hard from the impact, but he sprang back up immediately. He heard growls and the scratch of paws, and he said softly, "Good boys! Good boys! Are you hungry? Want a snack?" It was all he could do to keep from yelping the words.

The dogs began to whine, and instead of biting him, they jumped up on him, planting their forefeet against his chest. He emptied the parcel, and he heard them snarfing up the bones and meat scraps.

With his hands stuck out in front like the Frankenstein monster in the old movies, Jarvey made his way across the lawn. He found the house, worked his way to the front door—if servants were still there, they'd be more likely to be in the back, he reasoned—and set to work with his picks.

He couldn't see a thing, not even the torchlight from the gatehouses a few yards behind him. It helped to close his eyes. He began to sweat as the pick found the lock pins and slowly moved them. The dogs came over, sniffing him, rubbing against him, probably hoping for another snack.

Jarvey began to sweat in frustration. Remembering the time he had used magic to force a lock open, he tried to hold back those feelings. Zoroaster had warned him that old Midion could sense magic. It wouldn't do to alert Nibs, not now, not when he was so close—Jarvey felt a click, another, and another. At last the pins all seemed free, and he gingerly reached to turn the knob. With a soft click, the latch opened, and Jarvey pushed inside the house, closing the door against the dark and the dogs behind him.

One gas light burned low and blue in the great

room. He found the door that led to old Tantalus's study. A lock secured it too, but an easier lock, and with a minute's attention, he had it open. Inside Hawk's anteroom, Jarvey risked turning up the gas a little. That let him open the last locked door, the one into Tantalus Midion's library. He stepped in.

It was safe enough. The big windows had been covered with heavy maroon velvet curtains. He shut the door behind him and turned up the gas.

So many books! Jarvey went to the desk and pulled a large open volume toward him. It was in some foreign tongue, all swirls and squiggles, and he couldn't read a syllable of it. He moved over to one of the two sets of shelves and looked at the spines. Some of the books were old and crumbling, some fresh with gilt lettering. None had titles that sounded at all helpful. Maybe the other shelves—

He was in the middle of the room when the door boomed open. "Thief!" shrieked a shrill voice.

Jarvey spun, numb with shock. Old Tantalus Midion stood in the doorway, his face a mask of rage.

Behind him, grinning wickedly, stood Charley Dobbins.

CHAPTER 13

The End of the World and What Happened Next

*M*idion lurched forward, his hands crooked into threatening claws. "I'll have you in the mills for life!" he shouted. "No! I'll burn you to ash in the town center at midday, as a lesson to others!"

"Told you you'd catch him red-handed, my lord," Charley said. "That's old Jarvis Green, that is!"

Jarvey dived past Midion, and Charley, laughing, jumped to block his escape. Jarvey had the satisfaction of delivering one punch to Charley's midsection that made the black-haired boy collapse before old Midion's surprisingly strong claws hauled him back. Midion almost threw him into the chair behind the desk. "So you're the snipe who I've been hearing of," the old man said. "Well, my friend, your games end here, tonight. You, Dobbins, run to the Holofernes station and fetch Captain Hawk. Now!"

Charley got up, stared fiercely at Jarvey for a second, then slunk away. Midion crossed his arms. "You think I am an old man, and you are young and strong. Do not deceive yourself, boy. I have the art, and I can deal with such as you by crooking a little finger."

"You've got the art," Jarvey bluffed, "but I've got the Grimoire."

Midion's face writhed. His shaggy white eyebrows bunched in a ferocious scowl. "What? Grimoire? Don't be a fool, Green."

"My name's not Green," Jarvey said. "It's Midion. Jarvis Midion."

The old man staggered as if hit by a blow. "Midion? Midion? It's not possible!"

"Look at me," Jarvey said, hoping his voice sounded braver than he felt. "Remember the old rhyme? Hair like rusty gold, eyes a midnight blue?"

"Nonsense!" Midion snapped. "I'll soon beat the truth out of your hide—"

"Do, and you'll never find out what happened to the Midion Grimoire," Jarvey said, gambling that the old man would believe him. "You've known something was wrong with your little kingdom for weeks, haven't you? Well, here's what's wrong. I came through the Grimoire to your Lunnon, and I brought the book with me."

"Here?" Midion screeched, and Jarvey heard real terror in the sound. "No, it can't be. You'll come with me!" One of his talonlike hands shot out and seized Jarvey, dragging him out of the chair. Midion marched him through the darkened house until he came to a tall, narrow door. Standing before it, the old man raised his free hand, clenched like a claw, and began to chant in a weird, singsong voice: *"Foris! Abra, abri, abrire!* I command it!"

The door did not open, but dissolved. Beyond it lay a swirling darkness, a whirlpool of fog and night. "That is living death, you snipe," old Midion said. "I have but to give you a push, a little, little push, and in you go, to be swallowed there. Death, did I say? No, death in life! There you will drift forever, aware, alone, and not even able to die, lost in darkness for all eternity! Shall I give you a little push, my lad?"

Jarvey's voice shook: "Go ahead if you never want to find the Grimoire."

With an animal bellow of anger, Midion dropped his hand, and the door stood as before, solid. "I'll learn your secrets, and when I know all you know, I may be merciful and merely throw you through the dark gate. Or I might do something even worse to you!"

Bread and water and loneliness. They came to be all Jarvey knew, locked in a windowless room on the second floor of the palace. Sometimes old Midion would appear to ask if he'd changed his mind yet. Jarvey refused even to answer. Time and time again he tried to work some magic to open the locked door. It refused to budge. Curled in a ball of hopelessness on the floor, Jarvey passed the time by dreaming up ways he could revenge himself against good old Charley.

None of them would work, but they passed the time.

At last Jarvey became aware that the interval between meals had stretched on and on. His throat was dry, and his empty stomach clenched. He dully wondered if old Midion had decided just to let him starve.

His mind drifted, and it clutched at something that floated by: that strange word, *abrire*. Old Tantalus had chanted it before the magical doorway, but he had heard it chanted before. It was one of the words—he was almost sure it was—that Siyamon

Midion had said just before the Grimoire pulled him in. If he could only remember the other. If he could only . . . he drifted in and out of strange dreams.

The clicking of the lock wakened him. He braced himself. Midion must be coming back to make his demands and his threats again. The door swung open, the yellow light spilling in painful to Jarvey's eyes—

"You're a sight," a familiar voice said. "Ready to get out of this, are you, cully?"

Jarvey sprang up, tottered, nearly collapsed. "Betsy!"

"Sh! Come on. Old Nibs is out for the evening—Council's meeting and he's presiding as Lord Mayor and Dictator for Eternity. Come on!"

Jarvey staggered into the hall on unsteady legs, blinking in the light. Betsy wore a gray skirt and a white blouse and apron. A white bonnet covered her red hair, and her face was cleaner than he had ever seen it. "How did you get in?" he gasped.

Betsy rolled her eyes. "Thirty housemaids come in every day, Jarvey. Do you think anyone would notice a thirty-first, bringing up the rear?"

"Listen," Jarvey said urgently. "Charley's—what's the word? Peached on you."

"I know," she said grimly. "Don't worry about Charley. He's got himself in trouble, and he won't soon get out of it. The tippers have him in a cell right now, trying to pry knowledge out of him that he doesn't have."

"He said your father—he said your last name, Dare—"

"Yeah, I know," Betsy said. She led him down a corridor and through another door. "Come on."

"Can't leave," Jarvey muttered. "I have to get back to old Midion's study." He lowered his voice. "Where's the book?"

"In the pantry," Betsy said. "Tucked where no one's likely to look. I knew you were going to break into the palace, and I was afraid they'd find a way to force you to give it up so—I took it. I didn't want to trust it to anyone else. I've been carrying it with me everywhere for weeks."

"You brought it here?" he groaned. "You've got to get it. Is Hawk in the house?"

"No. He'll have gone to the Council with Nibs. He's become old Nibs's bodyguard since my— since Lord Zoroaster disappeared."

They reached the big domed front room. Betsy pressed something hard and cold into his hand. "Nipped this," she said. "You might find it useful."

It was an old-fashioned key, and it fit into the locks of both doors. Jarvey pulled the heavy maroon drapes across the windows of the study, turned up the lights, and frantically began to read through the titles of the books he had not been able to examine.

Enchantments. The Arte of Magick. Ye Practyse of Divers Artes. Which one, which one?

Then, at the end of one of the shelves, a row of small black books, no titles on their spines. He opened one and read in angular handwriting:

> . . . the spell is simple enough, with the Grimoire. I have found servants in plenty, desperate men who wish to be out of the way of the police and the queen's men. With them I will build my refuge, a London where I may rule . . .

A diary. Jarvey flipped through the pages, stopping to read a line here and there, but none of it helped. Most of it took the form of angry ramblings against fools and enemies. One shaky passage dealt with Tantalus's discovery of the date of his own approaching death: June 12, 1848. It ended with the words "I must escape this world before then."

Jarvey nearly jumped out of his skin when the door opened. But it was only Betsy, holding the Grimoire. "Here it is. Let's go!"

"Wait, wait. It won't do us any good unless—"

"We've got to go!" Betsy warned. "Nibs is always back before midnight, and it's gone half past eleven by now. Come on, there's no time!"

They raced into the big front room—

And the front door opened, freezing them in their tracks. "What!" An outraged Tantalus Midion glared at them. "You! I'll teach you to—"

"This way!" Jarvey yelled, and he ducked back down the corridor toward the library, slamming and locking the door behind him. He grabbed the heavy table that Captain Hawk used as a desk. "Help me!" Betsy took hold of the table, and they tugged and shoved, blocking the door.

They retreated into the inner study, and Jarvey locked that door as well. He heard a thunderous blast from outside. The house shook with it, and he reeled, the way he had teetered when old Siyamon had chanted out—

Abrire ultimas!

The phrase came back and as the door to the study bowed as if a giant's hand were pushing it, Jarvey snatched the Grimoire from Betsy's hands and shouted the words aloud.

The door opened—

A door of light, not darkness—

Everything was light.

White radiance flooded the world, and Jarvey could see only the figure of Betsy standing at his side. Before him reared another gray, indistinct figure, its features impossible to see in the white glow, but it had to be Tantalus Midion.

The book, the Grimoire, writhed in Jarvey's hands. It struggled to open.

"Fool! Fool!" Tantalus's voice, sounding distant, thin, tiny.

"To Earth," Jarvey yelled. "To London, and take

Tantalus Midion there!" Words of desperation, not art.

And he opened the Grimoire.

The universe went insane. Everything swirled, water going down a cosmic drain, falling away, down an endless whirlpool. Tantalus Midion swept past, blue eyes wide with terror. Away, away, screams fading.

Jarvey fought a wind that whipped at him, sucking him forward. The book struggled in his hands like a living thing, but he had to resist, had to find his parents.

A power greater than he could resist snatched at him, jerked his feet from under him. Jarvey yelled in despair, trying to hold on to the Grimoire, trying to fight the endless fall, knowing he lacked the power. He tumbled headfirst, toppling, unable to stop himself.

Something as strong as iron clamped onto his wrist, and a commanding voice shouted, *"Quietus!"*

Darkness and drifting, and then the feeling of something soft and yielding beneath him—a grassy hillside. "What happened?" Jarvey asked.

"You did a foolish thing," a voice answered from the darkness. "A foolish and brave thing."

"Who's that?"

"You know me as Zoroaster," the voice answered. Then it called out, "Elizabeth? Are you here as well?"

Someone lurched against Jarvey, and he heard Betsy gasp, "What happened? Where are we?"

"Not in Lunnon," Zoroaster said firmly. "And not back on Earth, where Tantalus Midion has gone. I believe we are in an unwritten chapter."

"An unwritten—" Jarvey broke off. "What about my mom and dad?"

"They are somewhere in this," Zoroaster said, and Jarvey felt something hard thrust against his chest. He closed his hands on the familiar shape of the Grimoire. "Let's have a little light," Zoroaster said, and immediately a soft blue-white glow surrounded them.

Jarvey gasped. Zoroaster was older, years older, than he had been a few weeks earlier. "What happened to you?"

"Travel," Zoroaster said. "Travel between the worlds of the Grimoire and the real world. I can slip back and forth, using my own magic. It may or may not surprise you to learn that Zoroaster is not my name, that I am a Midion too."

"So I am, too," Betsy whispered. "I'm your cousin, Jarvey."

"Wh-what?"

"Lord Zoroaster is my grandfather. My mother was—was—"

Zoroaster put his hand on her shoulder. "She was my only daughter. You see, back on Earth, I was Tantalus Midion's bitter enemy. He never actually met me, nor did he realize that my name was truly Midion, but he knew I opposed his evil plans and his use of the Grimoire. He had no hold on me, but he did kidnap my only daughter and force her to come to this terrible place. You see, he thought that if her life were in his power, then I would give up."

"But you came here——"

"I came here, yes. I took the name of an evil man who had helped Tantalus—but one, like me, whom he had never seen face-to-face. I came here not just to fight Tantalus Midion's magic, but to find and save my daughter." Zoroaster took a deep breath. "By the time I arrived, she had vanished into the crowds. For years I searched for her, while pretending to be one of Tantalus Midion's helpers. Until I found her, I was unable to face him openly, you see."

"Did you find her?" asked Jarvey.

"Too late," Zoroaster whispered. "I found her too late, not more than a year ago. In all that time, I never realized that she had been married to one of Tantalus's hated policemen. Her husband kept her practically a prisoner, until he made Tantalus angry at him. When Tantalus had the man punished, my daughter fled and went into hiding. By the time I found her—"

Betsy was crying. "She's dead," she said softly. "The note that my grandfather gave you led me to her grave. He was waiting there and explained things to me."

"Did Tantalus kill her?" Jarvey asked.

"No," Zoroaster said. "Despair did. The first Transports were immortal in Lunnon—unless they lost the will to live. When her daughter and her husband were taken from her, my Estella simply gave up and died. Possibly no one but a Midion could do that. Death is a way of escape, you know—the final, grimmest kind of escape. No one around her knew about her parentage, though. No one took particular notice of her death—not even Tantalus, who never knew that the man who became one of his advisors was the same one whose daughter he had stolen back on Earth."

"Here," Jarvey said, holding the Grimoire out. "Use this to find my parents. You promised."

Zoroaster sprang back, his expression shocked. "Don't tempt me with that cursed book! It would corrupt and ruin me, as it has others of our family."

"You promised!"

Turning his face away, Zoroaster said, "Listen, Jarvey: I cannot use the Grimoire because I have studied magic, and its power would change and warp me, turn my good intentions to evil ends. For weary years I have tried to put right the terrible wrongs my kin have done, but I cannot use the Grimoire to find your parents. You will have to find them."

"I don't know how!" Jarvey wailed. "And—and I'm afraid."

"I know you are. Our evil kinsman Siyamon will

try every spell he knows to find a way to the book. If he succeeds, you are lost. You have to master your art, Jarvey. I don't know how to advise you. Midions have always trained their own in the art, father to son. And they start when the son is much younger than you are. Your magic has awakened, but it lies under the surface. I can only tell you that you must keep the Grimoire safe, and that you must not use it, except to travel to where your parents are imprisoned in it."

"How do I do that?"

"I don't know," Zoroaster confessed, looking defeated. "All I can tell you is that you are a Midion, and if you use your art for good and not evil, you may have a chance."

"All alone?"

"Not alone," Betsy said. "I'm going to help."

"You can go back to Lunnon, though," Jarvey said. "If Zoroaster can get there, he can take you too."

"I can't," Zoroaster said. "The Grimoire might allow her passage, but no magic of mine would be safe for her. My spells will allow me to pass between worlds, but I survive only because my art protects me. I don't think that my art is strong enough to keep the passage from killing Elizabeth. The Grimoire could send her back, but I dare not use it."

Betsy's expression was determined. "I wouldn't go back to Lunnon anyway. There's nothing for me there now that I know I can't help my mother. And it'll be war, won't it? When the people learn that old Tantalus's magic no longer can destroy them, they'll rise against the Toffs. The Free Folk are better organized than the tippers know, and I think in the end there'll be a new Lunnon, one run fairer and freer than the old one. But it's their fight now, not mine. All that held me in Lunnon was trying to find my mother, and that's done with now."

"I must go back to Earth," Zoroaster said. "Siyamon Midion is a formidable enemy, worse even than Tantalus. I will have to fight him on that side while you keep the Grimoire safe." He paused. "I hope you can protect it without having its curse fall on you. You have some power, but you have not perfected it. The Grimoire has little hold on you. It is evil, though, the curse of the Midions. It will try to trick you and trap you, Jarvey. Still, if you hold on to your desire to free your parents, if you fight against the book's temptations, I think you have a chance."

Jarvey held the Grimoire and stared down at it, hating its unearthly texture, its deadly weight. The book gave him a chance.

It wasn't much, but it was all he had.

All? he wondered. No, not quite, because he had the Grimoire, and the desire to find and rescue his parents, and Betsy.

He had a chance, a hope, and a friend. Against

that stood the unknown, the threat of old Siyamon, and the curse of the Midions.

He raised his eyes and saw Zoroaster and Betsy looking at him.

"All right," he said. "We start right now."

THE END OF BOOK ONE